where he grew up during the Second World War. He studied Fine Art at Durham University, and Sculpture at the Slade in London, before teaching art in schools in the North of England. He was also branch director of the Samaritans, a journalist and an antique dealer. Between 1985 and his death in 1993, he retired to devote himself to his writing.

His first novel for children, *The Machine-Gunners*, published by Macmillan in 1975, won the Carnegie Medal. He won it again in 1982 for *The Scarecrows* (the first writer to win the medal twice), the Smarties Prize in 1989 for *Blitzcat*, and the Guardian Award in 1991 for *The Kingdom by the Sea*.

'A writer who managed to combine literary excellence with an immense talent for capturing the imagination and interest of child and, in particular, young adult readers.'
Independent

'Westall was a writer of rare talent. We shall miss him, but he has left us such a wonderful legacy.'
Michael Morpurgo, *Guardian*

Books by Robert Westall

Fiction
Blitz
Blitzcat
Blizzard
Break of Dark
The Call and
   Other Stories
The Cats of Seroster
The Christmas Cat
The Christmas Ghost
Christmas Spirit
The Creature in the Dark
The Devil on the Road
Echoes of War
Falling into Glory
Fathom Five
Fearful Lovers
Futuretrack Five
Ghost Abbey
Ghosts and Journeys
Gulf
Harvest
The Haunting of
   Chas McGill
If Cats Could Fly
The Kingdom by the Sea
Love Match
The Machine-Gunners

The Night Mare
Old Man on a Horse
A Place for Me
The Promise
Rachel and the Angel
The Scarecrows
Size Twelve
The Stones of
   Muncaster Cathedral
Stormsearch
A Time of Fire
Urn Burial
Voices in the Wind
A Walk on the Wild Side
The Watch House
The Wheatstone Pond
The Wind Eye
The Witness
Yaxley's Cat

For adults
Antique Dust

Non-Fiction
Cats' Whispers
   and Tales
Ghost Stories
Children of the Blitz

ROBERT WESTALL

Voices in the Wind

MACMILLAN
CHILDREN'S BOOKS

First published 1997 by Macmillan Children's Books

This edition published 1998 by Macmillan Children's Books
a division of Macmillan Publishers Ltd
25 Eccleston Place, London SW1W 9NF
and Basingstoke

Associated companies throughout the world

ISBN 0 330 35218 0

1 3 5 7 9 8 6 4 2

A CIP catalogue record for this book is available from
the British Library.

Printed and bound in Great Britain by Mackays of Chatham PLC, Kent

19882
FICTION

Contents

The Shepherd's Room	1
The German Ghost	33
Cathedral	51
The Bottle	70
The Return	79
Aunt Florrie	90
The Beach	105
Daddy-Long-Legs	122
The Trap	141
The White Cat	169

The Shepherd's Room

Pasture House may still stand today; a long sandstone building in the Pennine foothills, a mile from the village of Unthank. It wasn't really a house, in spite of its single chimney. It was a great barn, with twelve foot high doors to let the hay carts through. At one end, a disused cow-byre, where the transparent carcasses of flies still spun in the draughts, caught in the webs of long-dead spiders.

At the other end, up a narrow outside stair, was the room with the chimney. They called it 'the shepherd's room' though the farm no longer had a shepherd.

As a child on holiday with my parents, the shepherd's room fascinated me. Long and low and dark, with a single small window dingy brown with dust and cobwebs. The fireplace was just a hole in the gable, black with soot. The walls were whitewashed, but dark grey with the years. Hung with harness on rusty nails – harness so old the leather was like iron.

There was one three-legged stool. Otherwise, just that litter of yellow and blue chemical drums every farmer leaves lying around – quarter-full of paraffin, sheep-dip and nameless evil-smelling stuff.

1

A lonely place. The farmhands came once a year, for the sheep-shearing and dipping. Otherwise it was left to the wind and rain and the finches who hopped in and out of the great open doors in search of food, their cheeping shockingly shrill and noisy in the stony silence.

As a child, I spent hours there, in the shepherd's room; for the presence of the shepherd was still strong, as if he had just left it. I would sit on his stool and wonder what he had been called, and how his life had been. When I was grown-up, I would come and live here, and find out . . .

But what I did find out about was hate. And murder.

The weather brought the hate, and the murder. And the weather took it away again. It had nothing to do with me.

But the weather was lovely, as Alan and I climbed up to Pasture House. It was nearly Easter, 1950 or 1951, I forget which. And real seasonal Easter weather. It had been chilly when we left Newcastle; it was colder now, and I wondered vaguely what the weather forecast was. But every five minutes the sun came out, blessing your eyes with frail golden light and the back of your neck with that gentle warmth that brings out goose pimples. Primroses glimmered beneath the dark hawthorn hedge, and, higher up, stray daffodils blew at the base of drystone walls.

We kept our heads down, and panted, for we were heavy laden, with pans clanking beneath our rucksacks. Alan was already twenty yards behind, though his pack was lighter than mine. He kept shouting at me to wait for him; and moaning non-stop when I paused to let him catch up. Why the hell had I chosen *him*? Well, he'd been the only one who wanted to come. My usual mate, Big Dave, was caught up with his sister's wedding. And Alan seemed better than nothing. I'd often nattered to him in the prefects' room, waiting for my real mates to turn up. He was little and wiry, with bushy black eyebrows, sticky-out teeth and a face like a monkey. But he seemed pretty bright. He'd been good company on the trans-Pennine bus, and when we bought under-age drinks in the pub at Alston. It was only when we started to walk from the bus that I discovered he was a moaner. He'd just bought some industrial work-shoes with steel toecaps, and he said they made his feet hurt . . .

We'd called in on the farmer, who I knew well from the holidays with my parents. He'd given us a mug of tea in his warm farmhouse kitchen; and, as we left, said with his sly Cumberland grin which he always had on his face when talking to townies:

'You'll have a bit of company up there. I've turned my breeding ewes intut yard. Mek sure you close tut gate.'

'Right!'

'If weather turns a bit rough they can go intut barn. An' . . .'

'Yeah?'

'Keep an eye open for new-born lambs. Mek sure they're up on their feet. If they don't get up straight-away, they'll die, this weather. An' . . .'

'Yeah?' I said, a bit warily.

'If you see a ewe in trouble, run down an' fetch me, there's a good lad.'

What could I say but yes? No wonder he wasn't charging us any rent. We'd be his unpaid shepherds, saving him a two-mile walk, three times a day. He always was an idle sod . . .

'Right!'

But my heart was light, as we reached the stone wall round the big cobbled yard. All the ewes were on their feet, tearing at bales of hay against the wall. Or simply chewing the cud, staring at us with their weird oblong yellow eyes. We had to wade through them; like a wide warm woolly lake. You could feel their sharp little hoofs stepping on the toes of your boots. And the solid pugs of sheep-dung as you trod on them.

When we reached the stair, Alan began to moan about the sheep-dung caught in the tread of his shoes.

He didn't like the shepherd's room at all. He didn't like the way the door was only fastened by a chain, so it always hung an inch open. He didn't like the draughts, when the door was left wide open. He didn't like the darkness when it was shut. He wasted a lot of time trying to clean the window.

I said, 'It'll be a lot more cheerful when we get the fire going.'

He said, 'There's a bit of coal, but no wood.'

I got the hand-axe out of my rucksack and tossed it across to him. 'Plenty of wood yonder.'

Fifty yards away, across the field, was a fallen ash tree.

'What're *you* going to be doing?' he asked suspiciously.

'Trying to make us some mattresses.' There was a pile of big corn sacks in the corner. And plenty of hay in the yard, if I got to it before the sheep finished it.

Grumbling, he went.

Three corn sacks, full of hay, made a good mattress. I laid three each side of the fireplace.

After a bit, he came back with an armful of measly twigs.

'That'll last us all of five minutes,' I said.

'The axe is blunt. It just bounces off.'

'For God's sake,' I snarled, taking the axe off him. 'Didn't they teach you camping in the Scouts?'

'I didn't go camping. I had asthma.'

'Well, break up those twigs an' get a fire going.'

'There's no paper.'

'Use your *Manchester Guardian*.'

'I've not read it yet.'

Wordlessly, I got mine out of my rucksack and tossed it to him. 'An' don't use it all. We'll need some for the loo.'

'Where is the loo?'

'I haven't dug it yet.'

'I need to go now.'

'Well, use your imagination.'

I stamped off to the fallen ash tree. The axe *was* a bit blunt. But the tree was so dead you could snap big branches off with your bare hands. I smashed them into usable lengths by stamping on them.

Fastened them together with my belt, and carried half a tree home.

He'd done nothing but get a bit of a fire going. He was hunched over it, about a foot away. Ruining his eyes trying to read what was left of my *Manchester Guardian*.

'What about starting on the tea?'

'Fire's not hot enough yet.' His voice was full of grievance as if I'd done him an injury.

I didn't say anything. Just went and smashed the hell out of the ash tree and carried two more bundles home.

He was still sitting there. He hadn't moved an inch. The fire seemed no bigger.

'What about a brew-up?' I said. I was parched.

'No water.'

'There's a stream just outside the wall. Didn't you see it?'

'There's no bucket.'

I went to my open rucksack and tossed across a folding canvas bucket. American Army issue. I'd just bought it at the Army and Navy stores. He went, grudgingly, without a word.

I got out my tins of grub. It's always the same; they seem to weigh a ton when you're carrying them. But when you get them out, they don't seem much. Corned beef and spam; processed peas and baked beans. Still, there was a shop in the village. Spam and beans would do for tonight. I got out my army mess tins, and put a slab of lard in each.

'Hey, this bucket leaks . . .'

He stood dribbling water all over the floor. A dark tongue of it licked out towards my mattress.

'Get it out of here, for God's sake.'

He went and stood it at the top of the steps outside, where it steadily made all the steps wet. 'What you want to buy a leaky bucket for?' he asked peevishly.

''Cos it wasn't leaking when I bought it. Having no water in it. It'll probably go watertight once it's well soaked.'

'I doubt it,' he said in disgust. And just stood triumphantly watching the water running out of it.

It took him about ten minutes to work out he could fetch water in a mess tin. Just as well for him; otherwise he wouldn't have got a brew-up at all.

The next hour was comparatively cheerful. The place didn't look too bad, once we'd lit the old hurricane lamp that the farmer had left us. And unrolled our sleeping bags on to the mattresses. And the fire was really roaring up the chimney fit to roast you, and all our gear was spread about, making it really look like home. A lot better than the two-man tent Dave and I had had two weeks in, in the Cuillins, where you couldn't move for sweaty socks. But he kept saying how dirty the floorboards were, and scraping stuff off with his scout-knife to prove it. Or asking how we would get hot water to shave in the morning . . . But finally he shut up moaning, and even offered to wash out the mess tins in the stream, if I would give him some stuff to do it with.

'Use pebbles,' I said. 'Little pebbles. Or earth.'

He gave me a look like I was mad; but I gave him a look, and he went. It was like camping with a Girl

Guide; except a Girl Guide would have had compensations . . .

Still, I sat and toasted my legs, and nursed my bellyful of spam and beans, and had a fag, quite content.

And then old misery-guts was back.

'The sheep are acting peculiar. They're all packed into the barn like sardines. And the sky's a funny dark colour . . .'

'It's called *night*,' I said. 'Don't blame me for that. Blame God.'

'I wish you'd come and have a look at the sheep.'

I got up with a groan.

The sheep were behaving oddly. All packed densely together at the back of the barn, away from the door. I tried heaving one out to look at it, but it fought like a mad thing, so I let it go and it rammed itself straight back in.

'The sky's more than *dark*,' said Alan triumphantly from the door. 'Look at it. It's not *natural*.'

I came and looked. Across the Eden Valley, the mountains of Lakeland, in the last rays of the setting sun, looked as pale green and translucent as glass. Above them, and all round to the north-west and north, the sky was an awful purple black. It looked like an approaching cliff; it looked more solid than the earth. It looked like it was going to push the frail Lakeland hills over, and trample them underfoot. It was eerie, ghostly.

And I'd seen it once before.

'Oh, hell,' I said. 'A blizzard.'

And then the Lakeland hills were blotted out as if

they'd never been. And then the sun. I swear the temperature dropped ten degrees, from pretty cold to gut-wrenching freezing. And then it was night, black howling night. I could hear the wind coming, faint and shrill, like a pack of hounds in full cry.

'Let's go back down to the farm,' said Alan nervously.

'You wouldn't get a hundred yards. Help me get these barn doors shut.'

'Forget the sheep . . .'

'You idiot! If we don't get these doors shut, this wind'll take half the roof off.'

Dragging and heaving, swearing and yelling, we got the first half of the doors shut, and the big bolt in place, hammered well into the hole in the ground. The wind hit us as we got the other half shut. I just managed to get the chain fastened, when I heard another tree come down in the hedge where we got our wood, with a cracking rustling roar.

And then the wind slammed us against the doors. And on it, stinging, blinding, driving you mad with pain, hailstones as big as peas. Above us, the door of the shepherd's room was trying to beat itself off its hinges.

We crawled and groped up those outside steps. Luckily the gale kept us pinned to the wall. Any other direction, it would have blown us off.

It took two of us to shut the door. In the red light of the fire, the floor, our beds, were a mass of hailstones. The fire was leaping out from the fireplace in great clutching fists of flame. The top half of the room was full of whirling black smoke – even the old hurricane lamp had gone out. I relit it with trembling fingers, and we stared at each other in speechless horror as the old barn, with its two-foot walls, shuddered as the blasts hit it. And wave after wave of hailstones came under and round the chained-up door.

'Sacks,' I said. 'Stuff sacks round the door.'

At least the wind stopped our quarrelling. When the stuffed sacks were in place, we sat one each side of the fire and fed on more wood, and listened to the heavy slates creaking and shifting and grinding together overhead.

'They know we're here,' he whispered. 'The farmer's got a Land Rover . . .'

'Anybody moves outdoors tonight's a fool,' I said. 'There'll be deaths by morning. There were the last time. We're on our own, Sunny Jim. Till it stops.'

'This your idea of a holiday?' he said bitterly. 'I think you're barmy, that's what I think.'

Oh, God, there were tears in his eyes. I began thinking longingly about that Girl Guide again. As I said before, he had all a Girl Guide's faults, and none of her virtues.

That wind seemed to have the cunning of an animal. It felt its way in through chinks in the stonework, leaving little white fans of powdered snow. It sifted snow in through the creaking slates; it fell in a mistlike shower through the red firelight. It came up through the floorboards, making our mattresses rustle and move, as though they were full of mice.

But the cold was worse. We huddled as close to that great roaring fire as we could; till it burnt the sides of our faces unbearably. And yet still our sides away from the fire were freezing. Alan kept reaching inside his rucksack and fishing out his spare clothes and putting them on. Pyjamas, spare shirts, spare trousers, socks, just as they emerged. Soon he was as bulky as the Michelin man, and as ridiculous as a scarecrow. He pulled his balaclava down over his face, till he was no more than a pair of bushy eyebrows, a corpse-white nose and a pair of terrified eyes. And now he just said nothing. Not a bloody word.

I mean, if Dave had been with me, we'd have cursed and made bad jokes and laughed, and told each other what a good story it would make for the blokes, when we got back to school. But this one just sat and quivered like a jelly. And when you're scared yourself, a black miserable jelly is the last thing you want to be with. I wanted to reach over and punch him, just to get him to make a sound.

But instead, I brewed some tea; four sugars and lots of condensed milk in our pint enamel mugs. It seemed to revive him a bit, but all he said, all he mewed, was:

'It's so *cold*. I can't believe it's so *cold*.'

Then he went and dragged over all the remaining wood to his side of the fire. Crawled inside his sleeping bag and just sat. Putting wood on the fire as if it was the only thing in the world that was worth doing. He put more wood on his side of the fire than mine. I had a nasty suspicion he would have taken the whole fire off me, if that had been possible.

We drank a lot of tea, that night. Made by scraping the piled-up hailstones into the mess tin. At least we shouldn't be short of water, while the storm lasted. I think I cooked something, though I can't remember what. Otherwise we sat and listened to the hundred voices of the wind, and that little grinding as the roof slates shifted. And felt, through our bums, the way the barn shook. It made me feel very small, like an insect.

I think I despised him for taking to his sleeping bag at first. But then I dozed, and wakened to find my fingers had gone numb as boards. So I crawled into my sleeping bag too. Funny how the world had simplified. Warmth and roof and wind was all that mattered. I'd brought a Penguin book with me, my favourite, the poetry of T. S. Eliot. Now it was just something we might need to chuck on the fire ...

Suddenly he said in a tight voice, 'I need the loo! What shall I do?'

And I said, 'How the hell do I know?'

Then he leapt out of his sleeping bag, desperately fumbling at his numerous fly-buttons. And then steam was rising from a pool in the middle of the floor.

'Christ,' he said, unbelievingly. 'I've wet myself.'

I couldn't bring myself to speak to him. He'd reduced us to the level of a pigsty. I felt my first stab of *real* hate. I got up, and went along the row of yellow and blue drums the farmer had left, and weighed them one by one, till I found the emptiest. I used it myself, before I was caught the same way. We'd drunk too much tea, and the cold had killed all feeling. The smell of sheep-dip came up from the drum to my nostrils; well, it was better than the smell of pee. Then I dumped the drum beside him.

'*That's* the loo. In future *use* it; *before* you have to.'

On the way back to my sleeping bag, I slipped on the floorboards and nearly went headlong. His pool of pee was freezing already. Well, it would keep the smell down.

I never got warm; but I slept in the end, with my mittened hands down inside my crotch, and the sleeping bag pulled over my head. Nothing kept out the noise of the wind. I dreamed the wind and cold all night. Every so often I'd waken and peep out, bleary-eyed, and he'd just be sitting there, putting more wood on the fire.

I was wakened by him shaking my shoulder violently. A dim grey light was filtering through the window. What the hell was he going on about?

'There's no wood left. There's no wood left!'

'Go and get some, then!'

'You're better at it than I am. I'll keep the fire going.'

He was scraping up coal dust with his mittened hands, and throwing it on the vast heap of white ash, which still glowed red here and there, as the wind blew down the chimney. It just made a lot of smoke.

Bloody hell, I'd fetched enough wood yesterday to last a week! But there was only a scattering of twigs left . . .

I moved. Every bone in my body ached; the cold bit into the back of my neck, my waist, my wrists and ankles. But I moved. Picked up the axe and went to the door.

The wind had lessened. The snow had stopped, though from the look of the sky to the north-west, not for long.

It was piled two feet high against the door. It filled the yard in a sort of scoop-shape. Piled high against the walls, but in the middle of the yard the cobbles were clear.

Down the valley, every feature of the landscape was gone, rubbed out as if by an eraser. Except for the tops of trees and telegraph poles, white down one side. A mile away, there was a blur of dark smoke where the village was. I was just glad to know people were still alive. But as far as we were concerned, they might as well have been on the mountains of the moon. I somehow knew the blizzard wasn't finished and if I got caught halfway . . .

I had my first bright idea. Dug out the useless bucket he'd left on top of the steps, packed it with snow and dragged it inside. If the blizzard did come back, at least we wouldn't be drinking floor-scrapings . . . Then I began kicking the rest of the snow off the top step. I'd nearly got it clear when my legs suddenly went from under me, my knees hit the edge excruciatingly and I nosedived twelve feet. Fortunately into a four-foot drift. Gasping with shock, with half the drift down the back of my neck, I got up. All that hurt was my knees. His scared face peered down at me.

'You all right?' He didn't sound concerned, he sounded aggrieved. Like I was a bit of useful machinery that might have broken down.

'That stupid bucket. You left it there, leaking. The steps are a mass of black ice.'

'How was I to know?' It came out as a self-pitying wail. He didn't even say sorry; and he might have killed me. I felt like strangling him, or at least swearing at him non-stop for about ten minutes. But one look at the sky told me that would be a luxury I couldn't afford.

I picked the axe out of its hole in the drift, and trampled my way through the drift to the ash tree. Trampling relieved my feelings; especially as I was sure that under all my clothes my knees were bleeding; hot little trickles kept running down my shins.

I took it out on the ash tree as well. It was easy; the branches were brittle with frost. I made a bundle so big and long I could hardly carry it.

He had the door chained shut when I got back, of course. And he wasn't watching out for me. Gone back to his sleeping bag, no doubt. I had to shout four times before he answered.

'Grab this! Haul it up!'

'These branches are too long!'

'*You* break them. Exercise will do you good. And steady on putting wood on the fire . . .'

I got another bundle the same size. As I was going back for a third, the sky to the north-west began going back to night. The next blizzard was on its way. But if I was quick . . . I wanted that third bundle more than I've ever wanted anything in my life.

I was on my way back when it hit me. Just knocked me flat and when I got up the whole world was just hailstones. I couldn't open my eyes, I couldn't even breathe. Every time I opened my mouth the wind sucked the air out of my lungs. Then it knocked me flat again. And again. I didn't know which way I was facing. There were little icicles on my eyebrows and on the front of my hair lashing my forehead in the wind. My mind was a whirling white panic . . .

Only one thing saved me. The trench my feet had punched through the drift. I crawled along it. But was I crawling to the barn, or back to the tree? And the trench itself was rapidly filling up with blown snow. And my hands were like planks of wood again . . . I wondered vaguely if I was going to die. But it really didn't seem to matter any more.

Then, suddenly, the loom of the barn. I crawled up the steps whimpering to myself in a comforting sort of way. I shouted and shouted at the little bastard to open the door. Was he going to leave me there on my hands and knees to freeze to death?

Then the door opened, and I crawled into what seemed like warm still darkness.

'Haven't you got more wood?' he asked.

I got to my feet and stared aghast. He'd let the fire go out. He'd jammed a lot of wet logs on, and they just lay on top of the white ash. There wasn't a flicker of flame.

I think I went mad then. No more warmth, no more hot tea, no more light than one measly hurricane lamp. It was the end; and after all I'd done . . .'

I ran along the row of blue and yellow drums. Till I

found one that stank of TVO. Tractor vaporizing oil. What they run the tractor's diesel on. I took off the screw top, and threw the contents at the fire. The lot.

There was the most enormous flash and bang. Fire shot up to the ceiling. An arc of flame came shooting out towards the mouth of my empty drum. I had the sense to drop it just in time. There was another explosion inside the drum. Hot air flashed past my face, and I felt my eyebrows and hair crackle. Burning hair smells horrible.

But, glory, we had a fire again. The logs were roaring up the chimney. God bless TVO. I just stood there and laughed. Like a maniac.

I looked and he was cowering in the corner.

'You're *potty*,' he said, his voice full of hate.

I noticed he'd only bothered to smash up two or three of the branches. Keeping close to the fire to do it, so that all the snow and bark from them was scattered over *my* sleeping bag.

'Get breaking them branches,' I said. 'If you let the fire go out, I'll have to do that again. There's *plenty* of TVO.'

'What about cooking some breakfast?' I asked at last. I didn't think for a moment he would. I just wanted to hear what excuse he would make.

'My hands are too numb to work the tin-opener . . . and they're bleeding with that wood . . .' He held up hands so black you couldn't see the blood. 'Anyway, *you're* the cook . . . so *you* say!'

Aha, his young lordship was getting stroppy again.

I wondered how he'd react if I punched him or kicked him. Probably just collapse into an even more useless heap.

So I just said, 'Boil some water for tea.'

'There *isn't* any water.'

'There's snow in the bucket.'

'There's black stuff mixed in with it. We could get *ill*.'

'Go out and get some clean stuff, if you're that fussy.'

He used the stuff in the bucket.

'Why don't they come for us?'

'Because they've got better things to do,' I said savagely.

He looked at my face. I realized he'd become really afraid of me. It didn't make me feel sorry for him. Just more like hitting him.

Still, I cooked his breakfast. Or rather I just cooked a lot, and shovelled a bit less than half onto his dirty plate, and sent it skimming across the dirty floor to him.

'Manners!' he said petulantly. Did he know how much he was chancing his arm?

Still, I felt a lot better after I'd eaten. Animals always do ... And then the blizzard stopped again. My last bundle of branches wasn't quite buried, and I nipped out and rescued it.

'And I want that lot snapped up, before I get back!' I said.

'You're very good at giving orders! Who made you camp-commandant of Auschwitz?' Then he stopped looking defiant, and looked worried instead. 'Where you going?'

'Only to look at the ewes.'

I opened one of the big double-doors gingerly; glad it opened inward, and not outward against the drift. There was a flurry of panic among the ewes, as I closed the door behind me, and stood to let my eyes get accustomed to the dark. The ewes ran to and fro, cannoning into me, and nearly knocking me full length into their droppings. After a bit, they quietened down and began baaing. And there were some shrill treble baas among the deeper ones.

There was some light in the place, from narrow slits in the walls high up. As my eyes got used to it, I could see tiny lambs moving beside their mothers. One, two, three, four, five, and they were all legs and head, and little bits of what looked like bloodstained string hanging down from their pipe-cleaner bellies. What a night they'd chosen to come! Still, they were up on their feet.

At least... the ones I could see were. But... I began to search the filthy cobbled floor with an uneasy twinge of guilt.

And in the end, I found it.

It looked like a tiny rug, so flat it was, on the frozen floor. A little woolly bloody rug, with the knob of the head sticking up at one end, and four pathetic trails of legs. It was *so* flat, as if it had melted into the floor, as if the floor had sucked its life away. Its eyes were glazed and dusty. Its mouth was open a little. I knew it was dead without having to touch it. I couldn't believe it had ever been alive. It only seemed half the size of the living lambs.

I just stood and stared. I'd done that. I'd let it die. Ended before it was begun. And I had promised to keep an eye open . . .

I felt like a criminal. If the real shepherd had been in his room, he'd have done his rounds with his lantern. He'd have saved it. Whereas I had snored on, sleeping bag over my head. It must have cried out, as its life drained away, and I had never heard. I picked it up, prizing it off the floor, stiff as a board, and put it in the corner, where the others wouldn't trample on it. And I took a vow then, that no more lambs would die.

Then I turned to see the ewes clustering round the closed door. The blizzard had stopped, and they were hungry.

There was plenty of hay across the yard; under the drift. Maybe the ewes could dig it out . . .

Then I knew I was thinking stupid. If the ewes went out, the lambs would follow. Into that bitter wind . . . I wasn't going to risk that.

The hay must come to them.

I drove them back from the door with shouts and kicks. Two ewes got past me as the door opened, but no lambs with them. I slammed the door on the rest and fastened the chain.

The hay might be under a drift, but those two ewes soon found it. Shoving aside the snow with their noses, they were soon munching contentedly. Actually, the drift that side was mainly hay. It lay in the lee of the wall.

I pulled out a couple of bales, by their baling wire. Two of us could lift them easily.

'Hey!' I shouted. 'Give us a hand!'

At my fourth shout, he opened the door a crack. And said in his cross peevish voice:

'What do you want *now*?'

'Give us a hand with this hay.'

'What do we want it for?'

'It's not for us. It's for the sheep.'

'Never mind the sheep. That's the farmer's job. That's what he's paid for.'

'C'mon. It's good exercise. It'll get you warm.'

'I'm warm here. I've got to watch the fire.'

'You mingy little creep!' I really saw red then. I ran across and up the steps, meaning to drag him out by main force.

He slammed the door shut, and I heard the chain go on.

'Sod off. Leave me alone.'

'Open this bloody door.'

'Get lost.' Through the crack I saw him walk back to the fire and get back into his sleeping bag.

It drove me berserk. There he was, sitting burning the wood I'd paid so dear for, and the cold was starting to eat into my bones. And I kept giving fearful glances at the sky. The blizzard might start again, at any moment. I called him every filthy name under the sun. I tried to wrench the door open by main force, but it was too strong. I was starting to lose all control, starting to want to plead with him.

'Not so big now, are you, Stubbins?' he called. 'Go back to your sheep, if you're so fond of them. Or take

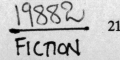

a little walk down to the farm . . .' He was loving it. He laughed. At me. The little rat.

I wouldn't give him the satisfaction. I decided to let him sweat. I'd better get up a damned good sweat myself. I was getting slow and sluggish with the cold.

I got five bales across in the end. Piled up one on top of another, as a barrier against the sheep. Then opened the door and quickly pushed the top one through, and slammed the door again. I put my ear to the wood. There was the satisfying sound of ewes tearing and munching.

I gave them three bales in all. In between, just to keep warm and alive, I went and smashed off a lot more branches and dragged them back. Broke them up. While he watched me sneakily from his little window, and laughed. And I watched the darkening sky . . . and grew really afraid.

I reckoned he'd let me in, in the end. After he'd reduced me to pleading, or maybe even weeping.

If only the farmer would come. With his great-wheeled tractor; and a can of hot tea. And some bacon sandwiches.

Stop fantasizing!

And then I saw the power of fantasy . . .

I waited till he was watching me again, then I pretended to see somebody coming up the track from the farm. I waved frantically. I even grinned with joy. He couldn't see the track from his window, see? I jumped up and down with delight. Then shouted, 'Hallo, Jack. You took your time coming!' To my non-existent farmer . . .

That did it. The door chain rattled, the door was

flung open. The little rat nearly broke his neck, in his hurry to get down his own ice-laden steps; his face alight with the delights of returning to civilization.

He stood beside me. Then he gave me a baffled, then a dawning look.

'*Where's* the farmer?'

'Here!' I said, tapping my chest.

He made a bolt back upstairs. I caught him by one foot, and dragged him all the way down again. He lashed out at me wildly, even tried to bite the hand that was holding him.

I gave him a push into the middle a snowdrift, and ran upstairs and chained the door against him. And watched for the blizzard coming back . . .

That brought him hammering and beating on the door. At first he just thought I was having a game with him. Then the cold began to get to him, and he began to plead, to offer me money, and finally to cry.

What a disgusting inhuman object!

It was then the temptation came. If I kept the door shut, said a little voice, I should be shot of him for good. All his moaning, sneering treachery. He wasn't fit to live. And when he was found dead, who could blame *me*? I could just say he started off down to the farm, and was caught by the blizzard. It was that easy. Murder by blizzard was the perfect murder. My head spun with a wild excitement; with an intoxicating sense of power.

And then I thought of the silence that would fall, after his last pleading was done, after his last feeble blow on the door. Then, *he* would have the power. I would have him on my mind, strangling me, blighting everything I did, for the rest of my life. Even if I didn't crack up under the police questions, the lawyers at the inquest, the look on his parents' faces . . .

He would make the very nastiest kind of ghost . . .

I couldn't get that door open fast enough. I had to drag him into the room, and dump him on his sleeping bag.

He crawled inside, and hunched over the fire.

'You were going to leave me,' he said. 'You were going to let me freeze to death.'

'Oh, no,' I said, as blithely as I could. 'I was just showing you how it felt. Never you *dare* do that to me again.'

His eyes were like black frozen marbles.

'Just give me the chance,' he said. 'Just give me the chance.'

So we just sat in our sleeping bags and hated each other, while the blizzard howled its endless song.

It eased, about five in the evening; by my watch that was miraculously still going. There was even a break in the cloud to the west and a glimmer of late sunlight, and I saw the hills of Lakeland, pristine and unsullied, under snow.

I began to worry about the lambs again. But if I went to inspect them, I knew what he would do.

Finally, I said, '*We're* going to inspect the lambs. Together. Then I'll cook you some tea.' It was like talking to a child; a mad hating child.

'Get lost.'

'You're coming, if I have to *drag* you.' He was so

much smaller than me; and weaker. Puny, really. But strong enough to chain the door on me.

And I was rather afraid of what would happen if I did lay hands on him, and began to push him around. My muscles were so full of rage, I mightn't be able to stop . . .

'Don't make me *drag* you.'

In the end, I pulled him to his feet. He resisted, his muscles like clenched wire. He clung to each side of the doorway. I simply pushed him off the top step, into the snowdrift. When he got up, spitting and cursing, and trying to get snow out from the back of his neck, I said, 'Go and stand by the barn door.'

He stood defying me a long time, then he began to get really cold and gave in. I followed him, watching him like a hawk, every step.

'Unchain the door. Push in that top bale. Now go in yourself.' I began to realize how prison warders must feel; or attendants in a hospital for dangerous lunatics.

I followed him in, and chained up the door.

'Go and stand against the far wall.' I had to give him another push. Then he went.

The barn was a bit lighter, with that sunset coming in through the western slits. There were a good dozen lambs scurrying around with their mothers, by that time.

But another bloody, woolly bundle on the cold cobbles.

Except, thank God, this one gave a weak bleat, and stirred, feebly.

'Pick it up.'

'It's *filthy*.'

'So are you. Pick it up. Or I'll leave you in here with it.'

I backed towards the door, through the munching sheep and over the half-eaten hay bale . . . I got out back through the door, and began to close it.

Only then did he realize how much I cared about the lamb, and how little about him. Given the choice, I think I'd have saved the lamb.

'I'll get my clothes all—'

'Pick it *up*!'

He picked it up and came out. I put the chain on, keeping between him and the shepherd's room. Then I backed up the outside steps.

Once they were through, I chained the door behind them.

He threw the lamb down on the floor, as hard as he could.

'It's shit all down me anorak.' It had too – a great green streak of diarrhoea.

Laugh? I thought I'd never stop. I think I only stopped because I was worried about the lamb. I carried it to the pile of old sacks and rubbed it dry with one. Then sat cuddling it carefully, so I didn't get diarrhoea down my front as well. I thought, for a long time, it was making no progress. I feared that in spite of all my efforts, it was going to die like the other one. I dipped my fingers in the tin of condensed milk, and shoved them against its mouth. But it wouldn't suck. I had never cared for anything in the world like I cared for that lamb. Never grieved at life slipping away before.

'It's going to *die*,' he said triumphantly. 'It's no bloody use.'

'Drop dead.' I stroked the lamb with my other hand, talked to it, crooned to it like a mother.

And suddenly, it gave a wriggle, and struggled to its feet, hind legs first. Suddenly, it was sucking at my fingers.

I laughed aloud in triumph.

'It's going to *live*,' I said, with hate.

I was still near the door, on those old sacks. He'd gone back to crouching over the fire, feeding it with too much wood again, so it was an inferno.

The lamb finished sucking the last of the condensed milk off my fingers. It felt OK. I started to get up.

Nobody had told me that a newborn lamb can run as soon as it can stand. It doesn't need teaching; it can run better than you or me. And nobody had told me that newborn lambs have no sense at all.

The moment I let it go, it ran straight for the heart of that roaring fire.

'*Stop* it!' He could have stopped it so easily.

He never moved.

It was lucky I played rugby. Before I knew what I was doing, I'd launched myself full-length.

I just caught a tuft of its tail. Hauled it back by half an inch of fraying wool. There was that horrible stench of burning . . .

But when I examined it frantically, it seemed all right. I think it had just burnt the wool on one foot. It limped a bit, but not much.

'We could do wi' a bit of roast lamb.' He laughed nastily.

'Time it was back with its mother.'

'Take it, then!'

'No, you take it. An if you drop it before it gets back to its mother, I'll punch a hole in you.'

And so we spent that night. Both awake. The hating shepherds.

The blizzard came back three times. But we went down to the ewes every hour, with that old flickering lantern. We rescued and managed to revive two lambs that would have died, else. I brewed a lot of tea. We ate up the last of our dwindling provisions. He opened a jar of marmalade and ate it straight, with a spoon. Cold does that to you; you get this craving for sugar. He ate his and I ate mine. We didn't offer each other anything. And we listened to the storm, and wondered how much longer it could possibly last, our ears and minds deadened by the endless noise.

But we never slept, only dozed, one each side of the fire, the way a real shepherd would've done.

You don't sleep, when somebody hates you the way we hated each other.

It was the silence that jolted me out of my last doze.

No wind.

Sunlight streaming in through our dirty little window. I ran and opened the door, and the air wasn't freezing, just fresh, almost warm. And the sky was blue from horizon to horizon. And the whole world was white and perfect.

And around Pasture House, animals.

Five bullocks, with long icicles dangling from the hair of their flanks. A horse, with a canvas jacket, comically white all down one side. Three sheep, their thick coats tinkling with ice. Even rabbits, and, in the distance, sitting on top of a swept-bare hillock, a red fox.

All in a half-circle, staring at Pasture House, staring at me.

What did they all *want*?

Man. Food.

Wild with a strange delight, I leapt from the stairs, and ran to greet them. Whooping, because cold and death and hate were gone, and the whole world was re-made. I ran to the hay bales by the wall, dug into the snow with my bare filthy hands, ripped up handfuls of hay and threw it over the wall.

The bullocks came, and the horse, and the sheep. Avid, big, steaming-breathed, jostling. I continued to throw hay, shouting to them so that the rabbits hovered, and old fox sloped away.

I am the good shepherd, I thought wildly. I am the good shepherd! I loved the whole world . . . except . . .

He stood on the top step, sneering down at me. He was packed. His rucksack was already on his back.

'The drifts . . .' I protested.

'I'll take my chance,' he said. Meaning: anything's better than *you*.

'I don't know why you bothered to come,' I said. 'If you dislike camping-out so much.'

'I *admired* you,' he said. 'I wanted to get to know you better.' It came out like a curse. And he never

29

said another thing. Just started picking his way across the parts of the field where the snow was shallowest.

I followed his slow progress through my grandmother's old opera-glasses, halfway to the village. Was I actually *worried* about him?

I checked the barn; there were three more live lambs, and no more dead ones. The ewes, growing crafty, charged the door as I was closing it again, and got out to the hay, which they exposed and demolished with great vigour. I left them. I wasn't worried about them now. The sun was almost hot; the air balmy. I knew the storm wasn't coming back. I was starting to forget what it had been like, already. The mind is a wonderful self-cleansing machine . . .

There was nothing left to eat but the browning nub-end of a tin of Spam, and the makings of one cup of tea. I was famished, but I hung on. I knew Jack the farmer would be up, sooner or later.

About midday, I saw the big blue tractor snorting its way up through the drifts of the track. He waved as he came, and I waved back.

'You managed then? I knew you would. I thought two bright lads like you wouldn't come to any harm. She's a good un, Pasture House. Seen off more storms than you've had hot breakfasts. And she'll still be seeing 'em off when you and I are pushin' up daisies.' He gave me his crafty know-it-all dishonest smile.

'We saved three lambs,' I said shortly. 'One died.'

'Aye,' he said. 'That's the way it goes. Three out o' four's not bad. I browt you a bit o' snap.' He handed me a greasy packet of his wife's bacon butties. I began to wolf them down.

'Three fellers dead in the Lake District,' he added, with an overtone of satisfaction. 'Climbers. Townies. They're fetching them down this morning, off Scafell. It was on the radio.'

I just nodded. My mouth was full of glorious food.

'Your mate's had enough of the country life, then? I gave him a cup of tea, but he wouldn't linger. He's off to the pub at Melmerby, to wait for the four o'clock bus.'

'If there is a four o'clock bus,' I said, huffily.

'Aye, there will be. Snowploughs are out, on the Alston road.' He pointed up at the great blue-shadowed bulk of Hartside Height. 'They'll have reached the Helmwind Café, up top, b'now.'

Then he turned and looked at me.

'Fancy staying on here, keepin' an eye to the sheep, now you've got the hang of it?'

'No,' I said. 'I don't think so.'

'Three quid a week, an' all the grub you can eat? And I'll run you up a bag of coal on the tractor . . .'

'No, Jack, I'd better be off.'

'Missing your mate?' He gave me another knowing grin.

It made me wonder. After all that hate, could I possibly be *missing* him? Or was I just sick of the stinking dark hell-hole Pasture House had become?

'Aye, well,' I said. 'I'll get me things.'

'If you're quick, I'll give you a lift down on the tractor.'

31

It was embarrassing. We had to travel back on the same bus. But he sat in the front and I sat right at the back; as far apart as possible. But I watched him, as he watched the great sweeps of snow-clad fell slipping past the bus windows into the dusk. And wondered what he was thinking.

As I wondered when I saw him in the prefects' room, the next term, smart, beautifully pressed, clean white shirt, laughing with his mates.

But I never got to find out. We never spoke again. Just watched each other, as we passed in corridors.

The German Ghost

Ghosts? I only saw one once.

If it wasn't a ghost, it was something worse.

It was during my National Service in Germany. Keeping the world safe for democracy with a typewriter.

Nothing dashing or romantic; spent most of my time sitting in an office in Sennelager. Snug, though. The central heating worked right through those bitter North German winters. Installed by Germans of course.

You could especially forget romance. Lili Marlene had long since given up hanging round the lamplight by the barrack gate; gone to set up some posh brothel in Hamburg with mirrors on the ceiling. And on a corporal's pay I couldn't even compete with Turkish immigrant workers, let alone Yank top-sergeants. I settled for the YMCA ping-pong table, the NAAFI and the movies.

Snug. Till the chinless wonders at HQ BAOR had the great idea of holding an exercise in the middle of January. 'Exercise Topknot', which we immediately christened 'Exercise Top Nit'. Usual old story – Russian hordes pouring across the Elbe onto the

North German Plain, and we were supposed to move into position to stop them.

'Move into position'. Sounds so simple. Reach your map reference point, camouflage your vehicles, dig your slit-trenches and put up your pup-tents. No Russki artillery pounding away at you; no MiGs strafing you at rooftop height. Just the endless winter fog that blankets the North German plain; the North German water that oozes into your slit-trench the moment you start to dig it; and the North German wind that drives sleet through every chink in your tent.

And it didn't help, knowing that the Russki hordes had far more sense and were no doubt toasting their stockinged feet round barrackroom stoves, and getting sloshed on cut-price vodka.

Or the fact that our vehicles were worn-out crap from the War. We had half-tracks from the Western Desert that couldn't manage five miles along summer roads without their tracks coming off or their engines dying of advanced emphysema.

And exercises are bloody *dangerous*. Blokes get killed. Not hundreds like in war, but they're just as dead. Squashed flat in their sleeping bags by tanks whose brakes have failed, having been parked for the night on a one-in-five slope. Killed by speed-happy army drivers trying to catch up with their convoys by driving their Humber thirty-hundredweights at ninety along the autobahn in a blizzard. Frozen to death in their pup-tents . . .

Stay alive; keep warm; have a brew-up. Those were my military objectives. After I'd been loaded into a

canvas-topped three-tonner with my typewriter and
filing cabinets, by a mob of foul-mouthed Jock
linemen from Glasgow, who wondered loudly why I
couldn't do my own loading.

At least I was with mates; they say while you have
fags and mates the bastards can't grind you down. Nil
carborundum. My main mate was Second Lieutenant
Roger Pratt, of the Security Troop. Also National
Service, and also a graduate. We'd done officer
training together; only he'd passed out and got his
little pip, and I'd failed through nipping off for a crafty
weekend in London and leaving my rifle concealed
(not very well) under my mattress. Roger envied me
my two stripes, and leisurely dinners of eggs, beans
and chips in the NAAFI. He said I was top of my pile
of crap, and he was bottom of his, in the Officers'
Mess. Everyone was bloody horrible to him, because
he was National Service and wanted to be a poet
when he grew up. The Army, above the rank of
graduate corporal, does not recognize the existence
of poetry. If the CO had caught Roger writing his
poetry he would have been court-martialled for being
idle on parade.

Anyway, we set off into the fog of war; Roger's
Land Rover and wireless CV truck in front, and my
three-tonner behind. We were lumped together
because we were both bloody useless, and nobody
wanted us getting in the way. My only job was to type
out Squadron Orders and file bumf from the War
Office, and Roger's job was to listen in to the radio
networks, to make sure that bored operators weren't
sending each other the words of dirty songs like

Eskimo Nell in Morse code. Roger and I reckoned that these dirty songs in Morse were our only chance of stopping the real Russkis, if they were invaded. By the time they'd been translated, and the Russian High Command had worked out what they were and stopped laughing, their whole campaign to conquer Europe would've ground to a halt . . .

Roger in front. Doing the map-reading. Roger couldn't read a map for toffee. He always got lost. Well, for God's sake, he was a poet, wasn't he? How could he make up his lines about 'the cathedral silence of the German mist' and read a map as well? And it was more than his pip was worth to ask any other British troops where we were. It would get back, with many a merry laugh in many an Officers' Mess, to our bastard of a CO. And then poor Rog would be for it.

That was where I came in. My degree was in German; I could ask German civilians the way . . .

But it suited me at the moment to sit by my driver in the warm cab with my own map. Probably half the division was lost by this time; the half who hadn't broken down.

Fog and flatness and old snow lying in ditches, and those endless bloody fir trees. Roger finally stopped and came back to me shivering in his officer's greatcoat.

'We're lost.'

'I think we're OK,' I said comfortingly. 'Just keep following this road till you come to a church on the left. We dig in by the church. The church is your map reference.'

'Do you think so?' he asked, trusting as a child. 'There's no sign of the rest of our lot . . .'

'It's them that's bloody lost,' I said firmly. 'Just look out for the church.'

We drove on; and, amazingly, a church appeared on the left. In the middle of a dense clump of pines, just right for us to hide our vehicles from air-observation by the Russkis, if there had been any Russkis and there hadn't been any fog. The church was an odd little place, with a tower with a sort of onion dome, the kind some Germans like. It had a graveyard too, full of rusting Gothic railings, tall tombs and long dead grass.

What it didn't have, which it should have had, according to the map, was a village attached. But I told Roger it was probably hidden by the fog ...

Anyway, my blokes and his blokes were making ominous noises about dying of exposure and needing a brew-up. And his wireless ops said they were getting the divisional operators' dirty songs through loud and clear, which was all that mattered to Security Troop. And Roger was convinced that if we went any further we'd only get more lost, and probably end up exchanging fire with East German border guards.

So we drove our vehicles in under the pines, and covered them with camouflage netting and dead branches; and dug our slit-trenches and watched them fill up with good old muddy German water ... The tea was strong and tasted great.

Two hours later, our squadron commander turned up in his Austin Champ, with the sergeant major sitting alongside. Unlike the CO, who was a miserable old bastard, our major was a real hero. Western Desert campaign, and a DSO at El Hamma. One of those blokes who has everything. Bright. Handsome as Errol Flynn, though he had to shave twice a day or his jowl went black. Real charm, even with the meanest squaddie; must have been a killer with the ladies. And he actually loved what he called 'real soldiering'. No matter how wet and cold he was, and even when one of his three-tonners was upside down in a ditch at midnight, he loved it all. He roared in now, driving himself like a maniac, with his terrified driver in the back cuddling his enthralled Labrador.

'You're out of position, Mr Pratt,' he bawled at poor Roger.

Roger turned pale. 'By how much, sir?' he quavered.

The major laughed wolfishly, 'About a hundred yards.'

Roger wiped his face with relief. He'd been expecting about ten miles ... a hundred yards was nothing in this man's army.

'This church is the old Marienburgerkirche. The new one's just down the road. Nearly fooled us as well, didn't it, sar'nt major?'

'Yessir.'

'This is actually a better position. More cover. Other place was a damned public football pitch ... which is no doubt why you chose this, Mr Pratt?'

'Yessir.'

The major smiled wolfishly again. Loving every moment, like a boy on holiday. The sar'nt major only managed a small frozen smirk. He was an old hand, only months from demob, and you could tell he felt the cold. He was wrapped up in everything he could lay his hands on, including a balaclava that must have been left over from the Murmansk campaign of 1919.

The major made a small alteration on the map strapped to his thigh, glanced keenly at our slit-trenches full to the brim, the pup-tents starting to flap loose in the wind. Then he looked at the church.

'Church looks all right to me – why the hell did they want to build a new one? And the graveyard's very untidy – that's not like the Hun . . . Still, carry on, Mr Pratt.' He zoomed away, splattering us all with mud, but especially Roger's new greatcoat.

We brewed up again, using a fire-bucket of sand soused in petrol. Another old Western Desert trick, but in that wind nothing more modern would work.

After that it just got murkier and more boring. Rog's operators kept logging the dirty song transmissions from the warmth of their CV, which had the luxury of closable doors. In my truck, I tried to knock out Squadron Orders with hands turning blue inside fingerless mittens. A few dispatch riders roared up, plastered with mud from head to foot so that bits of drying soil fell off their faces when they grinned. Like the major, they were loving it, breaking all speed limits to carry vital messages like:

'Amendment to Army Council Instructions. For "Army Spotting planes – aircrews" read "Army Spotting planes – airscrews".'

Roger kept me company in the cold, because I was

the only one he could share his innermost thoughts with. The only thing the rest of his troop ever discussed was who was the greatest centre-forward England ever had.

He kept looking over the tailgate and shivering.

'Funny-looking old church. Don't blame them for building a new one up the road.'

'Graveyard's full up, I expect. Standing room in the aisles only.' I wasn't feeling like a philosophical discussion. I was trying to work out who to put on orderly corporal tomorrow, and deciding it should be Masher Higgins because I hated him, and being twenty-four hours on orderly corporal the day you come off an exercise is a fate worse than death.

'Don't say things like that,' said Roger, with a poetic quiver. 'There's an awful lot of tombs. By the end, the dead must have outnumbered the living congregation . . .'

He dropped over the tailgate, and went and walked all round the building. When he came back, he looked less cheerful than ever.

'There isn't even a slate missing from the roof. But the windows are all dust and cobwebs. You can't see a thing inside . . .'

That was a mistake. He'd sort of given permission to inspect the church. And the idle ones in our mob, the runners and drivers, including that notable loony Spud Malone, left with nothing to do, had climbed the churchyard wall, and were wading through the long sodden grass between the tombs, and kicking at the rusty iron railings around the graves. I heard Spud yell something about Dracula and the next minute he was trying to bury his teeth in Taffy Williams' neck. Which was his mistake because Taffy, who's a big lad, punched him in the gut, and they both fell inside a set of grave railings.

'You'd better have a word with them,' I said to Roger.

'Oh, it's just high spirits. They're bored. They've got to let off steam somehow.'

By that time, they were letting off steam on a life-size marble angel, which by some quirk of the sculptor's art, was *remarkably* well endowed.

'Wouldn't mind a crack at you, darlin', when I get through the Pearly Gates,' said Taffy Williams, embracing her.

'Get your skiving hands off her,' shouted Spud Malone. 'I saw her first. Din' I, darlin'?'

The statue rocked alarmingly on its base, with a sharp grating sound.

'I really do think you ought to have a word with them, Rog. You know what the Germans are like about compensation . . .'

'It's all right. They're moving on.'

You must think we were a right pair of seven-stone weaklings, a second lieutenant and a full corporal, just letting them run amok, without opening our mouths. The trouble was, they were Regulars, and we were only National Service. To a Regular, stripes on a National Serviceman aren't worth the cloth they're sewn on; and a National Service pip is pure fancy dress. And we were a long way from the regiment. Rub up Regulars the wrong way, and they're quite likely to thump you one, and cheerfully do a month in the glasshouse afterwards. It was all a matter of pride. To them we weren't real soldiers at all.

We went on watching, hoping their boyish enthusiasm would find a new course, like an argument about whether Newcastle United should really have won the FA cup in 1922, followed by a fist fight.

Then they noticed the tall black marble tomb with classical columns down the front, and a gilded urn on top . . .

'It's the entrance to a crypt,' shouted Spud. 'Look, these doors open. They're only fastened by a chain.'

'Halloo, Drac,' bawled Taffy Williams, hammering with his fists on the metal doors. 'Howzabout dropping down to the local bloodbank for a pint?'

They hauled savagely on the doors, making the chain rattle and echo, harsh and sharp, through the dense pine trees. There were shouts.

'Bodies down there, in lead coffins.'

'Get the crowbar from the Land Rover.'

I muttered, 'Roger, for God's sake. If this gets back to the CO . . .'

He rose to his feet, with the pale resolution of a Christian martyr . . .

But he was too late. There was a new figure, standing between the church and the tomb. A figure all in black; in a kind of long black skirt. The sort some priests wear, with lots of little cloth buttons down the front. His head was bare, his hair was snowy white, and his dark eyes were blazing.

'Cripes,' said Roger. 'The priest. That's torn it.' We watched in horror.

'What's he saying to them?' asked Rog, after a bit.

'British scum. Murderers of German children. Defilers of German womanhood. Who won't even respect the dead . . .'

'It's lucky none of them speak German,' said Roger. 'They might thump him.'

'I don't think so. They're bloody paralysed. Even Malone.'

And indeed, I'd never seen our mob so totally cowed. They just stood like little children, while the harsh high German voice echoed and re-echoed through the grove of pines.

'We'd better go over and apologize,' said Rog. 'I think he's going to complain to the authorities. You interpret, right?'

We jumped out of the lorry, and made our way awkwardly through the long wet grass and tomb railings. We really had to look where we were going, or we'd have gone arse over tip. So I was only able to look at our German once we'd arrived. But I saw him quite clearly in detail, starting with his cracked black shoes, his greasy cassock, with what looked like fag ash in its folds, though it might just have been white dust.

I saw his white hands clenched by his sides, whiter at the knuckles; his droopy-folded neck; his white face marbled with little veins; his yellowing false teeth, as he opened his mouth to blast us in turn; and his fanatical dark eyes, that seemed to look right through your skull. I dropped my own eyes quick but the harsh voice went on and on and on.

Then I watched his cracked shoes stalking away, pressing down the wet grass.

'What did he say to me?' asked Rog.

'He said you weren't fit to be an officer. In the German army, you would have been shot.'

'I expect I would,' said Rog unhappily. 'Do you reckon he *is* going to make a complaint?'

'I never bet on certainties.'

I've never spent a more wretched night. OK, it was cold and wet and pitch dark. But I'd been cold, wet and in the dark plenty of times since I'd joined this man's army. And we were all safely inside the trucks. It would have been certain death in the tents, most of which blew down by morning.

Roger and I settled in the cab of my truck. The three drivers were in the cab of the CV, and the rest were in the back of the CV with the operators, who stayed on the air all night. And who no doubt were gossiping between themselves, making out that Roger and I were a pair of queers shacked up together.

We had greatcoats and blankets, and we could run the engine for a bit of heat, if the cold got too bad. We'd had three brew-ups with something stronger in them, and there were plenty of doorstep corned beef sandwiches. But the tea had tasted like ditchwater, and the sandwiches like cardboard, and the cold just kept worming its way in under the doors, through the gaps round the clutch and brake pedals. It seemed more than ordinary cold. When we did run the engine, we didn't seem to get hot air, just petrol fumes.

And that was before Spud Malone went for a pee. First thing we knew of it was when a dark figure ran slap into our cab, and began scrabbling at Roger's door like a mad thing. Roger grabbed his torch and shone it, and there was Malone's white distorted face. Lit from below by the torch, it looked like something out of hell.

All of a shake, Roger wound down the window.

'What's the matter, Malone?'

'Aah went for a pee in the churchyard. An' he was there watching me.'

'Who?'

'That nutter in black. I was half finished, and he was suddenly there alongside me. Made me piss all down me trousers.'

'Serve you right,' said Roger snappishly. 'Why did you have to go in his churchyard? You could've gone anywhere. You could be on a charge for that.'

'Thanks for nowt,' shouted Malone. 'He's not *human*, that feller. You can't hear him coming. He's still watching us now. Over there by the churchyard wall.'

Malone's teeth were chattering. I'd never heard teeth chatter like that before.

Roger switched on the truck's headlights. They showed the churchyard wall, the tops of the tombs, the pines. Was that a white face watching us? Or just a trick of the headlights? Whatever it was, when I looked again, it was gone.

And we couldn't keep the headlights on all night, without risking running down the battery.

'He's an effing Nazi nutter,' shouted Malone. 'I'd like to bash his face in.'

But the moment Rog switched the headlights off,

he was frantically scrambling into the safety of the other cab.

In spite of all the tea we'd drunk, nobody else ventured far from the trucks that night. They came out to pee against the truck wheels in twos and threes, with the headlights glaring. The thought of that creep suddenly appearing at your shoulder while you were relieving yourself was totally unnerving.

In between, Roger worried about the complaint that would go to the CO in the morning.

'He's bound to complain now. He's a fanatic. Staying up all night to watch what we do . . .'

We didn't get a wink of sleep till dawn.

We were less than a credit to Her Majesty's Forces.

Roger was a very *variable* coward.

As the darkness totally retreated, about eight o'clock, and he sipped his first brew-up of the day, his fear of ghosties and ghoulies and things that go bump in the night retreated, to be replaced by a growing fear about what our dear Commanding Officer was going to do to him, on receipt of a complaint.

The Germans were terrible in those days: they would lodge a complaint if you dropped a fag packet in the street. They would throw long-dead chickens and piglets in front of our convoys, so they could claim we'd run them over and get compensation.

After we got the message from HQ that we were pulling out at noon, Rog spent half an hour trying to shave in lukewarm water, then announced he was going down to the village to make a full and abject apology. He was even thinking of offering them a few Deutschmarks for their organ fund appeal, if they had one. I refused to contribute. Second lieutenants got more pay than corporals; though not much more.

But I went along to interpret. What had we got to lose? Mind you, I wasn't exactly looking forward to it. Having my lugs burnt off by the priest, then getting back to camp and getting my lugs burnt off again by the CO. And maybe losing a stripe, and the seven and sixpence pay that went with it.

The village was just round the first bend in the road; a neat tidy little place; very German, no litter. The new church was a modern brick job, with strange geometrical windows and a flat roof, and the priest's house was right next to it. We walked up the neat garden path like two prisoners going to execution.

The door was opened by a plump smiling little housekeeper, whose rosy face belied the gloom of her black dress. I explained what we wanted.

'Come in, come in,' she said. 'Father Koenig is just back from saying Mass. He is having his breakfast. I am sure he will want you to have coffee with him. Go through. I will fetch more coffee.' She pointed through to a door.

Roger knocked, and a voice with a mouthful of food called, 'Komm!'

He was sitting in front of a bowl of steaming coffee, with his snowy-white napkin tucked into his dog collar, and he looked up with a beaming smile.

A little round balding man, with rimless glasses and a very sweet expression.

Not the same bloke at all.

He said, in near-perfect English, 'Come in, gentlemen. I am always delighted to entertain our NATO allies. You must join me in some coffee.'

He got to his feet and shook hands with us both. His hand was warm and soft.

The housekeeper bustled in with fresh coffee as we sat down, then he said, 'What can I do for you gentlemen?'

Well, that was a bit of a facer, I can tell you. Roger blurted out a garbled version of events, and said he was sorry for what we'd done in the churchyard.

The little man frowned, baffled, and looked out of the window towards his new church.

'But you haven't been near my churchyard . . .'

'Not this one,' said Roger. 'The one up the road.'

The little priest went a shade paler. His hand, holding his coffee spoon, began to tremble. Then he stirred his coffee with endless, needless vigour, and watched himself doing it, intently.

'The *old* churchyard! Was any harm done to the tombs?'

'No. They only rattled the door of the black one. But the grass is a bit trampled . . .'

'So,' said the little man, still stirring, and a bit breathless. 'What is a bit of grass between allies? Nobody goes to the old church now. Even the relatives of those buried there are now dead.'

'The other priest seemed pretty narked . . .' said Roger, starting to relax a bit.

'My friend, *what* other priest? There *is* no other priest. There is only me, and I work alone. This is only a small village.'

He sounded so jovial, so reasonable. So why were beads of sweat breaking out on his smooth-shaved upper lip?

'*Him*,' I said, pointing. For I had caught sight of him, behind the little man's shoulder. The same black cassock and cracked black shoes; the same dark fanatical glare.

The little priest swivelled in his chair, very reluctantly, to follow my pointing finger. Then he turned back to us, and tried another smile. But it was as faltering as a creaky old theatre curtain going up.

'The photograph? That is Father Schalken, my predecessor.'

'Well he's still hanging round the church, and he's *very* angry.'

'My dear young man! That's impossible. He . . .' The little man faltered, and turned again to stare out of the window.

'He what . . .?' I asked. I think I knew already, but I had to know for certain. I'd have gone mad, if I hadn't known for certain.

'He was killed twelve years ago. In the bombing of Hamburg, while caring for the injured children. His body was brought back here and buried in . . .'

'The black tomb? The tomb with the urn on top?'

The little man nodded wordlessly.

'God, a ghost . . .' said Roger, shattered, and yet not entirely displeased. It's the poet in him.

'He *wasn't* a ghost,' I said. 'He can't have been. I saw the grass bending under his feet, as he walked away.'

The little man still tried to smile. But his face

seemed to fade away, behind the smile. His rosy cheeks faded to a network of little red veins, in a dead white face. As if he himself was the dead man, hovering on the verge of dissolution, frantically still trying to go on existing. He opened his mouth three times to say something. Then he fainted clean away, where he sat.

The housekeeper heard our yells for help, and came bustling in and took charge of him. As she loosened his collar and chafed his hands, she kept up a babble of German about the good father working too hard, and being under strain . . .

Roger and I got out, as he started to come round. I don't think either of us wanted to harm him further.

We got back to the trucks. I had never heard Roger give orders to break camp so decisively. And none of the Regulars gave him a moment's trouble. I had never seen men work so hard and fast. In twenty minutes we were setting up on the public football pitch by the new church. Right bang on the map reference this time. Again, nobody grumbled.

I remarked on this to Taffy Williams, my driver, once we were settled.

'It was that old geezer,' he said. 'He watched us right to the end. He might have thought he was hidden, but *I* saw him, among the trees.'

I didn't say a word. I didn't want to panic a whole army.

Cathedral

I should never have played the Virgin Mary.

I'm not even a Christian; nothing, really.

But when your father's Dean of the cathedral, Christianity is sort of the family business. You have obligations, unless you're a little bitch who likes making her father's life hell, and I hope I'm not *that* sort. Men like to think that clergy daughters are either frozen virgins or nymphos; but I just like a good time.

Pat Snow should've played the Virgin. I know she prayed for it beforehand, and cried when she didn't get it. She had a sweet little choirgirl-of-the-year sort of voice, and a figure like a sack (which would've suited the part). But she looks a bit like a frog, whereas everyone thinks I've got a spiritual look.

Now let's get this straight. I do *not* have a spiritual look. I do not *wish* to look spiritual. It's just that my father has a high forehead and wide-apart eyes and I take after him.

Which brings us to the Nativity Play, or rather the Cathedral Nativity Rock Opera. For we are a very with-it cathedral. My father wears collar and tie and sports coat most of the time, and Tony the Bishop's Chaplain goes in for jeans whenever he can get away with it, even though he has a fat bottom. Tony also reckons he is a poet, because he's had a few bits published in little poetry magazines. And his best mate is Nev, the assistant organist, who runs rock groups on the side, to eke out his pitiable salary.

Which is where the Nativity Rock Opera came from. Scheduled for early on Christmas Eve, in the cathedral itself. A big do, involving the cathedral choir; three rock groups; numerous junior-school choirs, sickeningly clean and combed and sat-on by their teachers; Tony, Nev and yours truly.

Why did I do it?

Well, I've got a big strong voice, and when you've got a strong voice, the cathedral becomes one great big echo chamber, a marvellous plaything. And they'd written a wonderful song just for me. Called 'Why Me?'

And there was no doubt it was going to be a big success, a sell-out, because they'd written other great numbers, like the Wise Men's 'Africa, Asia or Anywhere'. And the rock groups had set a lot of old favourite carols to a heavy rock beat, for the congregation to join in with. (In the manner of a Bach Oratorio, thus reviving an ancient tradition, as my father was quick to point out.)

I suppose I wanted to be a star. You don't often get the chance to be a star, in a little cathedral town like Sencaster.

And I was a star. The place was packed for the only performance (mainly with the parents of the junior-school choirs, I suspect). And the congregation really dug that heavy rock beat (when it was hallowed by carols) because they sang their heads off, and even clapped themselves afterwards. (Clapping in cathedrals is on, now, since the Pope's visit.)

And I really made that old cathedral ring, to its very furthest corners, with my echoes. That old cathedral and I really made sweet music together, like Stephane Grapelli and his violin.

Maybe that was the trouble; for cathedrals are strange beasts.

Or maybe it was Nev's wife's Christmas punch, at the party that they gave the grown-up (and semi-grown-up) members of the cast afterwards. We had to have it in the large clergy vestry, because it was late, and the restaurant in the cloisters was already locked up.

I remember that punch well; I shall remember it for the rest of my life. There can't have been much alcohol in it, the party being on sacred premises. But she'd put in everything from mint leaves to oregano, to try to give it some semblance of a kick.

Of course we were going on to a *real* party afterwards. With real booze. An all-night party, actually. My father didn't dig that much, on Christmas Eve. He'd rather have had me at Midnight Mass. But he owed me a favour, because I'd played the Virgin, so we both left any arguments unsaid.

Three different blokes had offered me lifts to the all-night party, and I hadn't quite made up my mind who to go with. The punch party in the vestry was just starting to wind up, and wind its scarves round its throats when, perhaps as a result of the aforesaid punch, I felt a sudden greasy queasy dagger strike me deep in my interior. I fled to the clergy loo, and spent a long time seated therein, staring at the odd cassock and surplice someone had left hanging on the back of the door.

You see, it was bad. Seriously incommoding. Not a gastric blizzard so much as a series of gastric squalls. Every time I thought it was over, it would start again.

I heard them, faintly, asking where I was. I heard them, faint and far off, calling my name. But I didn't worry. Someone would wait for me . . .

The last squall subsided. I wiped my bum, and, rather weak on my pins, staggered to the small clergy mirror, and decided I looked pale but interesting, and stayed to comb my hair and put on more lipstick.

Then I walked out; into pitch darkness. I grabbed backwards to put the toilet light on, and that switch clicked on total darkness too. Somebody, somewhere, had just switched the cathedral's mains power supply off. Even cathedrals are hard-up these days. Or maybe it had something to do with the fire insurance . . .

Somebody had *just* done it.

I screeched my head off, trying to make them hear. And in reply I heard a door bang shut with that thud and clink that all church doors make. Nobody had waited for me. Everybody had thought I'd gone to the all-night party with somebody else.

I was alone with the cathedral.

I told myself to stay calm. To stand still and let my eyes get used to the inky dark. No point in falling over something and adding a sprained ankle to my troubles.

It's amazing how your eyes slowly get used to the dark. First the big lancet windows of the vestry swam down at me, dark blue against black. Then the glimmer from the white formica table tops. Then a dark spiky huddle of stacked chairs.

But your eyes don't just get used to the dark; your ears get used to the silence, too . . .

I heard something approaching my hand along the nearest table top, which I was hanging on to for grim death. Something tiny and metallic; tiny footsteps, click, click, click. Dear God, what? A giant armoured spider? A rat on crutches? I gave a little yelp and pulled my hand away and hugged it with the other hand.

The clicking went on, but seemed to get no nearer. After a while, I grew bold, and felt out towards it. And my hand touched the warm smooth surface of a cooling electric kettle . . .

Idiot, I told myself. And groped through the door into the nave.

All the nave glimmered faintly in the dim orange glow of the street lamps outside the great windows. I could see right to the rose window at the far end. But it was the worst of lights. It lit up the backs of the rows of chairs, but it left all sorts of nasty black shadows in corners. And it made the stained glass windows, with their familiar pictures of saints look . . . unfamiliar. I suppose it was the reddy-orange of the street lamps. It turned the calm blues of heaven, the reassuring green of fields and trees into the reds and oranges and purples of . . .

I had really believed in hell when I was little. God was real to me then, and when God is real, so is the Devil.

I passed the window of St Peter raising Dorcas from the dead. St Peter had always been my favourite; with his curly white beard he reminded me of the retired sea captain who always spoke to my father after Matins, and gave me a sweet, when I was little.

St Peter was still watching me tonight; but I couldn't see the expression on his face.

But if the windows were bad, the carved statues were worse. They lurked all round the walls of the aisles, deep in their own shadows. The early bishops, lying flat, carved as flat and grim as stony kippers, on the boxes of their tombs . . . The later bishops that seemed to float upwards in a billow of marble clouds, cherubs and draperies. Those were the ones that used to make me giggle, they were so fat and pompous in their piety. But tonight I couldn't see their expressions; or their expressions were subtly different. As if they said, 'You have laughed at us all your life, my dear, but tonight is *our* time.'

I told myself it was just the strange way the light fell . . . Look how clearly it picked out that piece of lettering. Why, I could *read* it!

NEERE THIS PLACE IS INTERRED YE BODDY OF . . .

That was the worst moment. Of course I'd always known the dead were there; that the cathedral was as riddled with dark holes as a piece of Gorgonzola cheese, and that in every hole was a body in a lead coffin. My father had shown me some, once; when repairs were being done because the altar steps had begun to sag.

The strangest thing was that lead is not rigid, like a sheet of steel. Over the centuries, lead flows, droops. The lead of these coffins had drooped down on the skeletons beneath, as if they were no more than linen sheets. Every edge of every bone was visible; though my father said that probably the bones were crumbled to dust by this time, and the lead would flatten and flatten till in the end it covered . . . nothing.

Oh, yes, the dead were there all right. Nobody knew how many. Row upon row in the crypts beneath my feet. Stacked like forgotten books in some forgotten library, beneath the very stone slabs I was walking on. Were they listening to my footsteps pass?

They had always been there. But who remembers them while the cathedral's busy, and the organist is practising his voluntary, the vergers stacking hymn books, and the tourists flashing with their cameras?

I told myself not to be a morbid fool, and hurried towards the south transept door, which had a little door set in it; this was how we always got in and out when the cathedral was closed. It only had a Yale lock; one twist of the worn brass knob and I'd be out in the friendly bustle of Christmas Eve.

I reached the south transept door; reached up in the dark, with easy familiarity, for the worn knob.

My hand found a cold short lever instead, that would not move no matter how hard I twisted it. God, the new anti-burglar security. The cathedral contained many treasures, and a month ago there'd been a break-in and a sixteenth-century triptych and two Tudor chairs had been stolen from the Lady Chapel. This was a five-lever mortice lock, that would only turn, even from the inside, with a key.

There was no way out, till the head verger came to unlock the doors for Midnight Mass at half past eleven . . . Desperately I held my watch up, so the strange light from the windows caught it. Twenty past nine. It had been gone nine when I dashed for the loo. Had time *stopped*?

Then I remembered the phones. We have phones all over the place; for we are a *very* with-it cathedral. The nearest was in the head verger's office. I took a short cut across the chancel, trying not to look at the tiny point of red flame that hung above the high altar. This meant the Host was reserved there; the incarnate body of a God I no longer believed in . . . and yet the point of red light made me uneasy. If somebody had offered me a million pounds to blow that flame out, I could not have done it.

I did not want to look at it, there in the dark. But I looked, and saw it. Something made me. I just *had* to. Then I looked away again, where I was going. I wanted a sprained ankle now even less than I had in the vestry. With two good legs I could keep on the move, dodge dangers. But to lie helpless in the dark . . .

What dangers?

It was then that I saw it again; the red light from above the altar. Only now it had moved. Now it was floating in front of the pillar I was just approaching. Only ten yards away . . .

I didn't even stop to think; I blundered backwards in the darkness, terror rising like bile in my throat. When I looked again the red light was no longer there; it was floating in front of the next pillar instead.

A tiny click made me whirl. Now it was floating in front of the pillar behind me. And . . . click . . . there was another. There were three now, all round me.

I think it was only the tiny clicks that saved my sanity. How could anything Holy and Dreadful give tiny metallic clicks like . . .?

Our new infra-red burglar alarms, just fitted. I'd seen them often, in friends' houses. They clicked off and on when you moved, even in daylight, without setting the alarm off. But in the daylight, with friends, they were just a joke. We'd played games with them, waved our hands above our heads to make them click off and on.

I moved about now, making them switch off and on, listening to the clicks. They were not Holy and Dreadful; merely my obedient servants. I gave a rather wild giggle. They would be switched on tonight. An alarm bell would be ringing in the police station, in my own house. I would be rescued at any moment by my own father, followed by a mob of excited policemen. What a giggle!

But I still wanted a telephone. I wanted to hear my own mother's voice chiding me for my foolishness, while I waited.

When I got to the door of the verger's office, it was locked. More damned security . . . Oh well, there

was another phone in the cathedral shop, by the main
door. That was just behind wooden screens. They
couldn't lock that one away. I trailed down the centre
aisle of the nave.

Until I heard the voice. It was so low, so continuous,
that I doubted at first whether it was a voice at all; or
merely some other piece of machinery left running.

But I had to know one way or the other. In the
dark, you have to know, one way or the other. Or
you'd go potty. My heart in my mouth, on feet I tried
to keep silent, I crept towards it. The noise was
coming from the north aisle, and when I reached the
north aisle, it seemed to be coming from the tiny
Mountfield Chapel at the far end. And by this time,
I could tell it was human noise. A kind of babble.

The Mountfield Chapel is set aside for private
prayer and meditation.

Had I a fellow prisoner in the dark? How had he
evaded the vergers at closing time? Swallowing, I
crept nearer. It came to me that the babble was a
babble of grief. There was a sobbing in it. Who could
be sobbing on Christmas Eve? I'd always rather
avoided the Mountfield Chapel. I didn't approve of
people praying in public, except during services. I
thought them holy nuts at best, and attention-seekers
at worst. Mostly women.

But this was definitely a man. The weeping was
very dreadful and yet very human. I could hear the
ragged intakes of breath, blurred individual words. I
was sure it was a living man. And I determined
I would not let him weep like that, alone. Not on
Christmas Eve. Christmas was the time of good cheer.

I would show him sympathy, that there was always a bright side, if you looked hard enough for it. I would do him good. Then we would wait together for rescue to come.

The door to the Mountfield Chapel is extremely narrow. I put a hand to each side of it, and leaned my head through.

The strange orange light flooded in. There was a street lamp just outside the window. It seemed as light as day . . .

And the Mountfield Chapel was quite empty. It only held six chairs and a tiny altar and cross against the far wall. Nowhere for anyone to hide. And yet grief filled the place; echoed off the stone walls, assaulted my ears.

Oddly, I had no impulse to run away. I suppose I just knew there was nowhere to run to. I was here, alone, with everlasting grief. Instead, I felt a far-off anger; had the Church reduced some poor dead soul to such a state, with the burden of guilt it put on people? Madly, I even began to wish to comfort a ghost, to have mercy where God had none . . .

The voice, when it became clear, made me nearly jump out of my skin.

'Aah've been a bad bugger, a wicked bad bugger. Aah'll gan to hell an' burn . . .' It seemed right next to my ear. And yet I think I sensed there was something not quite ghostly, even before I heard the sound of vomiting. Even before I heard the sound of two sets of approaching footsteps outside, and saw two shadows of men cast on the window.

'Here he is! Jack? Jack? What ye doin' man? My

Gawd, he's spewing up against the cathedral wall. Ye can go to hell for that kind of thing, Jack! Didn't ye know that? You drunken old sot. Here, give us a hand wi' him, Stan. Let's get him home, the miserable old beggar. All that money poured away in drink, and he doesn't even enjoy himself . . .' The two shadows hauled another to its feet, and only then did I notice the open ventilator in the chapel window, low down.

My legs felt so weak, I sat down right there in the Mountfield Chapel, though I've always avoided the place. I tried a short scornful laugh, just to see if I could manage it. Nothing but a maudlin drunk!

Then I stopped laughing suddenly. A soul in torment was a dreadful thing; alive or dead; drunk or sober.

Meanwhile, there was the matter of the cathedral shop telephone.

But when I reached it, it too was dead. Cut off at the cathedral exchange, no doubt. Which was locked away in the head verger's office.

A numbness seemed to be coming over me. The cathedral, never warm in winter, now seemed icy as the last hot air effects of the congregation's singing at the Rock Opera wore off. I sat down in a pew, with my legs curled up under me, and under my coat, and my hands thrust up my opposite sleeves for warmth. My watch said ten more minutes had crept past on leaden feet. My father and our gallant police force were taking a hell of a long time getting here . . . Maybe the wonderful burglar alarm wasn't working yet. I tried blowing on my hands to warm them; it only made them damp.

I closed my eyes, thinking I might doze till the head verger ushered in Midnight Mass. Suddenly I had an overwhelming sense of someone tall standing over me, only inches away. I jerked open my eyelids and there was, gulpingly, no one there. And yet somehow I knew that if I let myself doze off again, my dreams would not be pleasant.

I must keep on the move. I must talk to old friends. For you cannot dwell all your childhood among tombs, without having your favourites.

Sir Rafe de Easenby; the great arch-tomb that blocked off a whole window of the south aisle.

Sir Rafe, according to cathedral records, had been a great and wealthy landowner of the thirteenth century. We still had the village of Easenby, five miles away.

Sir Rafe's wife had died in childbirth; along with his newborn only son. He had sold all the family estates and spent the lot on the great tomb. Then gone off and 'dyed in foreyne warres'. I was sure, as a child, that the 'foreyne warres' must have been a crusade. And it was so romantic; he must have loved his wife so much; not even thought of remarrying.

There they lay, in the glimmering orange light, amongst a great host of carved angels. Sir Rafe in full armour, with his crossed legs, and his mailed arm reaching across his body to draw his great sword. And his lady long and stiff with her many-buttoned bodice and wimple headdress. And the child, carved beneath them in his cross-banded swaddling clothes . . .

But they did not seem romantic tonight. They seemed a great scream of despair in stone. It was not a sane act, to spend all your living on one great tomb, before you died. It had shouted at God, at all Creation, 'They *will not* be forgotten, wiped out as if they'd never been.'

It shouted still, after seven hundred years. And I knew Sir Rafe had gone off to get himself killed. Suicide by holy war; a permissible suicide when any other would send your soul straight to hell . . .

As I stood staring, there came more noise from outside. I could spot when noises came from outside now. Besides, this could only be a sound of the present. Drunken young voices, laughing. Screeching music from a ghetto blaster, a cheap cocky confident girl's voice, singing over and over:

'It's got to be-heeee-heee *per-fect*,
It's got to beee-heee *per-fect*.'

You could tell from her falsely amorous tones that she was singing about sex.

Such brainless braying; such silly arrogance. What was ever perfect in this world? Sir Rafe knew the truth; and so did I. Then it seemed to me that these people laughing outside, were as insubstantial, as easily blown away, as a wisp of steam, as a used Kleenex blowing along the gutter. If there were ghosts, tonight, it was those people laughing outside. They would be annihilated for ever, once they passed out of earshot round the corner of the nave.

Whereas Sir Rafe was getting more real all the time . . .

In the end, his realness got too much for me. He

began to make me feel like a ghost too. I drifted away, towards Bishop Vavasour's pulpit.

Bishop Vavasour's pulpit was no longer used. It lingered dustily, behind a pillar, in the south aisle. It was carved with intricate medieval foliage. But, in the foliage, three dreadful flower-shaped scars. And in the middle of each scar, buried deep in the soft limestone so you had to wipe away the dust to see them, a round dark-grey mark.

Bullets. Round lead bullets that had once sat ready in the pistols of Oliver Cromwell's staff officers.

In 1647, one Sunday morning, General Cromwell, passing by, had called in to hear the sermon. Bishop Vavasour had been preaching a godly High Church sermon, a forbidden sermon, a Royalist sermon. Even after he had seen the General frown, Bishop Vavasour had continued his godly sermon. Cromwell, provoked beyond measure, had called on him to desist, in a bull-like voice that carried the length of the cathedral.

Bishop Vavasour had frowned at the unseemly interruption, and carried on. Cromwell had ordered his officers to draw and cock their pistols, then called on Bishop Vavasour to cease his blasphemy if he valued his life . . .

'What value is my life without my God, Master Cromwell? The cock shall not crow thrice for me . . .'

All three officers fired. All three missed. Perhaps the officers had tender consciences, and all aimed low, expecting another to kill the troublesome priest . . .

The Bishop continued to preach, dusting the stone-chips from his surplice. 'God has judged between us,

Master Cromwell. See the three new marks of the Trinity . . .'

'Throw him out,' shouted Cromwell. 'He shall not preach again.' But the Bishop continued to preach, as they bore him struggling down the aisle. A year later, he died, some say of starvation . . .

Another ghetto blaster came by. Rap, this time, echoing through the thin glass of the windows.

'Gotta get me a girl, gotta get me a drink,
If you think I'm evil, I'm what you think . . .'

Rap. Made up today; forgotten tomorrow.
Vavasour's pulpit, seven hundred years of stone.
Who are the ghosts, girl? Who are the ghosts?

It seemed to me that I was entirely absorbed into the cathedral now. As cold as its stones; as dried-out as the dust in the crypt. I no longer had any will of my own. I somehow knew I was walking to the base of the north-east tower. I just didn't know why. The whole place seemed as light as day, now, in the orange light from the windows. The saints watched from the stained glass as I passed, the floating bishops from their marble tombs. Far up in the roof, I could see the carved winged angels watching. And I knew that every one of the dead had an ear cocked to listen to my progress.

There is not much at the base of the north-east tower. They say it is the oldest part of the cathedral; and hardly anybody ever goes there. The walls are black greasy stone, mainly Norman work, and the windows are tiny.

The one thing there is, is an iron cart, a black thing

with huge spoked wheels like a Victorian pram. They used to lay the dead on it, in Victorian times, when they spent the night before burial laid out in the cathedral. I was afraid that *something* would make me lie on it . . .

But that wasn't what I was being led to. My attention was being drawn instead to the base of the wall. Where, more by memory than by sight tonight, I knew there was a herring-bone pattern of small narrow bricks, in a layer before the massive stones started.

The Saxons, long before the Normans, had used the herring-bone pattern. And they made it in Roman bricks, filched from the ruins of Roman villas long abandoned and ruined. They weren't good at quarrying stone, the Saxons; that's why they used anything that came to hand to build the first tiny church on our cathedral site. And in one brick is the pawmark left by a Roman cat. My father had showed it to me, when I was little. He said it was from the first century AD. And of course I believed him . . .

Like I believed in Bishop Vavasour and Sir Rafe de Easenby. Like I believed in the Saxons and the Romans. Like, for that matter, I believed in Julius Caesar, whose works I was struggling over in Latin in the sixth form at the grammar school . . .

But now I stood baffled. What did the cathedral want with me? I seemed to have come to a total halt. But all around the dead seemed to listen. Everything around me was the work of dead hands; even that little 1920s rush chair . . .

Out of the corner of my eye, I saw the little red

point of light above the high altar that seemed to me then the very eye of the cathedral.

Why had I accepted all the rest of history and yet rejected that red light? Why had I torn the red light out of the fabric of history?

Why are you rejecting me? asked the cathedral.

I don't know if I screamed at it out loud, or only in my mind. Because you're a *bully*, I shouted. Because you were built on the torn muscles and bloody bones of your builders; because your stone was bought with the money of the poor, so that their children starved. And you didn't *care*. And if I believed in you, you would start to eat *me*. Well, you're finished, finished, finished! People only come to *stare* at you now, because you're in the guidebooks. Soon, no one will believe in you. I don't believe in you; but I still hate you. I'm not a cringeing wet like Pat Snow, snivelling at her prayers. I'm going to be *free*!

It seemed to do the trick. The whole place became ... just an empty box. Like a disused warehouse. The stone was just stone and the glass was just glass, and the red light at the altar was no more to me than the flicking red eyes of the burglar alarm system. That was all. Empty nothing. One and a half hours of empty nothing, except the noise of the drunks reeling home outside, and the stupid songs they were singing and blasting on their ghetto blasters. An hour and a half during which I realized that nothing is the most frightening thing of all.

And then there was the creak and bang of the head verger coming in, his crisp footsteps in the aisle, the lights going on one after another, driving the darkness away with pools of pure gold. I hid from him behind the pillars; I had no intention of embarrassing either of us. And then as people began coming in for Midnight Mass, I slipped out unnoticed. Realizing I'd lost all taste for the all-night party, too.

But as I loitered, my father came hurrying up to the lighted door, his vestments over his arm. He looked a little tired, and a little worried, as usual. But his face lit up when he saw me, and he grinned and put his arm round my shoulders and said, just jokingly, and referring to my recent performance:

'Behold the handmaid of the Lord, be it unto me according to Thy word.'

I mean, being a Dean, he's always turning quotations from the Bible into little pleasant jokes. All our clergy do it all the time.

But this time, it went home like a spear. Be what you are. Say what you mean. Never pretend to be what you're not.

I'll never play at being the Virgin Mary again.

Not in that cathedral.

'Come to Midnight Mass,' my father said, 'since you seem to have abandoned your all-night party. Come to please *me*.'

And with a good heart, and his arm around me, I went.

To please him.

The Bottle

Mason knew the bottle was evil, the moment he saw it. As the bus braked sharply for the next stop, the bottle came rolling rudely from the back, and out between his feet, and into the space between the driver and the doors. It was a small chunky bottle of dark brown glass, with little glass dimples all over it. It had a vulgar yellow label; some kind of cheap fizzy soft drink, the kind kids loved.

As an ex-headmaster, the bottle aroused his ire. When on a school bus-trip, that was the point on the journey home when you knew discipline was about to break down, and chaos set in; when a pop bottle came rolling down from the back. That was the point where a good teacher stopped the bus, laid down the law in no uncertain fashion, and went up the aisle confiscating all the rubbish and putting it in a large polythene carrier bag. That bought peace for another twenty minutes; ten more miles nearer to home and domestic bliss.

Mason went as far as looking over his shoulder. He spotted the culprit straight away; a thin lanky boy with dirty washed-out denims, greasy hair and a slouching surly look on his face that seemed to have set permanently. Trouble with a capital T. But something warned Mason this was an ex-pupil, one of the Great Unemployed and looking for a chance to take it out on anybody. And not one of *his* ex-pupils, thank God. He reminded himself he was an ex-headmaster, early-retired; also one of the great army of unemployed. He told himself firmly to leave it alone. It was none of his business.

Still, ex-pupil and ex-head gave each other a certain look of recognition.

The bus started off again. The bottle came rolling back violently. Mason had to move his feet apart quickly, or the bottle would have hit him. It was humiliating to be made to hop about by a bottle. Again, he felt the thing was malignant. Then he told himself to cool off. That had been the whole point of retiring early; to cool off. County had been sorry to lose him; the parents – at least the solid majority of decent parents – had been sorry to lose him. Two of the younger women on the staff had wept. And he was only fifty-seven, with eight years to go. But his blood pressure was mounting inexorably each term, and he didn't need the money. His own kids had good jobs away from home, his mortgage was paid-up. The education officer had told him he was killing himself for nothing. His pension kept him and Sylvia comfortably. And the little antique shop he'd opened in Wedderby kept him in cigarettes . . .

The bus braked for the next stop. Mason heard the tormenting bottle start to roll forward again, and pushed his legs well apart while it rolled through. Then the scruffy youth passed him, coming down the aisle, grinning as if he understood perfectly. Mason and he exchanged one last glance of mutual hatred, the youth kicked mildly at the bottle, as if it were a pet animal being left behind, and got off the bus and slouched away round a corner, out of the whole business.

The bus started again. Mason eyed the bottle warily; but it seemed to have changed its behaviour. Now it rolled from side to side of the small distance between the driver and the bus steps, as the bus swung first to the left, then to the right. It seemed to have a will of its own, nosing into one corner after another, like a curious cat. It hung over the edge of the step. If it fell, it might break and leave a mess of broken glass, for passengers to trip and fall on. Mason had a fearsome respect for broken glass. There had been a corner of the playing field at his old school, which was never mown. One summer day, two boys were wrestling in the long grass and one pushed the other down on a broken bottle neither of them had spotted. The boy on the bottom, wearing only a shirt, had begun to scream; but the other had taken his screaming as part of the game . . .

Sixteen stitches and a punctured lung. Mason had never forgotten the journey to hospital in the ambulance, the blood spewing from the boy's mouth, every time they had to hold him down as they went round a sharp corner . . .

So Mason watched the bottle, like a rabbit hypnotized by a snake, waiting for it to fall and break. But it didn't. The raised metal strip on the edge of the step caught it and turned it back every time. For a moment, Mason hoped it might be a harmless plastic bottle. But it hit a seat with a loud clink; it was glass all right.

The only sound sensible thing to do was to go and pick it up, keep it in his hand and put it in the rubbish container when they reached the terminus. How often, in his career as a head, had he avoided accidents caused by other people's carelessness; the huge bottle of ink, balanced on the edge of a cupboard by a harassed young student teacher; an overturned broken chair on the stairs, just before the bell went. His staff used to say he could see an accident coming a mile away. For twenty years he had kept them safe, by foresight and nagging, vigilance and benevolent bullying. But that was what had made him ill. He was done with interfering with other people for their own good. In his little shop he bought and sold, as honestly as possible; he polished and dusted and watched the world go by with a keen but tolerant eye. As a result, his blood pressure was just a point above normal now . . .

He was still tempted to go and pick the bottle up. But the other people on the bus would stare at him, and the young driver think him interfering. Besides, stooping down made him dizzy and unsure and he didn't want to make a spectacle of himself. So he just sat and did nothing.

At the next stop, a youngish woman rose to get off. She had the hard set mouth and beautifully slim hard legs of a practised ballroom dancer.

As she approached the door, she trod on the rolling bottle without seeing it, and nearly fell; but recovered herself with ease. Mason heaved a sigh of relief. Now *she* would pick it up, now *she* would take it away.

And indeed, she went on and on and on to the driver, about the bottle. About how careless and irresponsible kids were today, and how her own fifteen-year-old . . .

Then she got off; without picking up the bottle.

Surely the driver, then . . .

And indeed the driver bent over and looked at the offending object. But he didn't open his little half-door and get out and pick it up. Instead, he just put the bus in gear and drove on. Too late, Mason realized how young he looked. In spite of his uniform, he had a spotty adolescent face and a semi-punk haircut. He wasn't what Mason expected of a bus driver; not a solid balding man of fifty, with hairy arms. Suddenly, Mason felt betrayed. Whose side were the bus drivers on these days? He felt as if someone had taken away a foundation stone from his already crumbling world.

The bus started up and drove on. A strong breeze roused Mason from his bitter reverie. The driver had left the folding doors of the bus open. It was, of course, against the rules. But bus drivers did do it in the hot weather; when it was really hot, it was quite pleasant, providing you weren't sitting on the front seat, where a sudden swerve of the bus could throw you through the open door; but it made the old ladies nervous; so they clung to their shopping bags with one elbow crooked round an upright pole.

But the breeze that was coming through the open doors was really quite chilly. Although the day was sunny, it wasn't that hot. What was the driver playing at? And why was the bus swaying about so violently?

Mason looked at the driver. The driver wasn't looking at the road ahead; he was looking at the bottle rolling around the bus. He was studying it so hard, he nearly went into a line of parked cars, only missing with a really wild swerve to the right at the last moment.

With that swerve, the bottle rolled to the very brink of the steps, and hung poised over the open door. On the point of falling out and smashing into the gutter.

Mason was on the point of crying out a warning, when he saw the driver was grinning to himself, as he watched the bottle. He was trying to get the bottle out of the bus. He would rather fill the gutter with broken glass than get off his backside to pick up a bottle. He was *playing*. A bus-full of adults was in the charge of a crazy reckless child in uniform . . .

Mason tried to get to his feet, and go and remonstrate with the foolish boy. But the bus was travelling at great speed now, swerving repeatedly, and Mason was afraid of getting dizzy and falling out of the open door. So he just sat on, in helpless horror. Just praying it would stop; that the bottle would not fall.

His prayers seemed to be answered. They came to another bus stop, and the lunatic had to pull up. After he started again, he seemed to have despaired of getting the bottle out of the open door. They were getting into the town where Mason lived now. They would soon be at the terminus. Then Mason could pick up the bottle himself and say 'excuse me' with heavy sarcasm, and put it ostentatiously into the nearest litter bin.

And then he saw the two cyclists. Two of his own. In the second year last year, so they must be in the third year this. Pew and Perry. Nice lads, but rogues. They weren't still wearing their uniform, though they were going home from school. They must have their blazers in their saddlebags. Their grey shirts were open-necked, so their ties must be in their pockets. And they were riding their bikes through the traffic like maniacs, one hand on the handlebars, pedalling so fast their legs were a blur. Foolish, foolish. I must raise the topic in assembly in the morning . . . Then he remembered he was retired; they were no longer his responsibility.

And just for a second, as the windows of the over-taking bus slid past the cycling boys, one by one, he relaxed into being the antique dealer, the one who no longer made judgements and laid down the law, who no longer forced his will on others for their own good. He saw the boys with the eye, not of authority, but with the eye of one who appreciates beauty.

And they were beautiful, their arms slim and brown, their faces tense and drugged with excitement, their eyes shining, their long hair blowing in the wind. He thought humbly that they looked like young gods. He thought sadly that he himself had never been like that. He had been a stolid cautious child who had never dared, never given his parents a moment's worry, never *lived*. And he had gone on that way all his life. Working in the library at university, when others had gone out drinking with the girls, he had got his safe second class degree. And so it had gone on; the young teacher whose register was always up to date; the diligent head whose prudence was praised by all. The man who was going home to a modest well-polished bungalow and a healthy, boring meal. Who had spent his lump sum on a shop, when colleagues had used it to tour Greece and Rome, or travel for a year with a mobile home through America.

All his life, he had said no, had missed the boat . . .

Too late, he came out of his reverie and saw the bottle, poised on the very brink of the step. As he raised a helpless arm, tried to shout a warning, it fell. He heard the crash of glass in the gutter. He heard the rear wheels of the bus crush the fragments of glass to smaller fragments. He swung round, looking out of the rear window, still desperately hoping to see Pew and Perry safe, far behind.

Instead, he saw Pew's face pucker up with terror, as his front wheel punctured and he lost control of his bike. Saw Pew swerve, out of control at twenty miles an hour, across to the far side of the road. Saw Pew vanish under the wheels of a furniture van.

The bus ran on; the driver seemed to have seen nothing. He didn't seem to have been looking in his rear mirror, didn't seem to have heard the squeal of the van's brakes. He swung right at the traffic lights and again swung right into the bus station as if nothing had happened. Turned off the bus ignition and walked away to the driver's rest-room, leaving the bus doors open so the passengers could get off in their own good time.

Very shakily, Mason got off the bus, and began to walk back to the scene of the accident. The sun was still shining warmly, and everyone was walking about quite as normal, so that for a few seconds, Mason's mind tried to pretend that nothing at all had happened; that it had all been an unpleasant daydream. But as he got further up London Road, people began to look over their shoulders, turn and walk back to where a large black furniture van was slewed right across the road. Then an ambulance came wailing past; and a fire engine, and the world was filled with the noise of their sirens.

A crowd had gathered, blocking the whole road. A young, white-faced policeman was already on the scene, trying to get them to move back. One look at the bobby's white face was enough to tell Mason the worst. He said;

'He's dead, is he?' All that youth, all that beauty . . . Pew had been the brightest boy in 2ad.

'I wish to God he was, sir,' said the bobby. And from the way he said 'sir' Mason knew that the bobby had also been one of his.

'It was the bottle,' said Mason. 'The damned bottle.'

The young bobby looked at him wonderingly. But he had other things to do . . .

The Return

The Suffragan Bishop of Tower Hamlets first noticed the steakhouse because of the sign on its roof. Driving past he looked up and saw in huge white letters:

THE COACHMANS

He tutted inwardly. It should be THE COACHMEN surely? His father had been a headmaster, and it had left its mark.

On his return journey, he saw another sign on the other side of the roof.

THE COACHMAN'S STEAKHOUSE

He nodded his approval. And because he was tired after a long and painful discussion with one of his clergy, whose wife had walked out on him, he suddenly drove into the car park and went in for refreshment. Only a cup of coffee, of course. It was a pricy place; not one a suffragan bishop could afford to eat steak at. Nor any poor coachman for that matter. When there *had* been coachmen, poor souls. Stuck up on top of their stagecoaches for hours in all weathers. For a moment, his mind drifted into a fret about the sufferings of the Victorian poor, then he pulled himself up sharply. He had enough to worry about with the present-day poor, without maundering on about those who were long out of their suffering. Poor clergy, so weary and overworked that their equally weary and overworked wives walked out on them. Poor children who came to London to make their fortunes and ended up as rent boys sleeping in cardboard boxes. The weight of the world's grief swept over him. But it was just the tiredness; a quick coffee would set him up, before the Deanery meeting about one-parent families.

The coffee, when it came, was good and hot. A nice big cup. The seating along the wall was soft; the lights dim, the tables, glistening with linen and silver, all empty before the evening rush. Peaceful. He nearly dozed off.

Until the yobs burst in. The Bishop shuddered at the tramp of heavy insulting feet, the raised, bullying discordant voices. He had tried to love groups of yobs on the prowl; he prayed often that he might be brought to love them; he still *loathed* them. Surely if Bishop Jim Wilson had learnt to love his Japanese torturers at Singapore in 1941 ...

He looked up reluctantly, desperately trying to bring a look of charity on to his face for these disturbers of the peace. It was instantly replaced by a look of shock. The yobs were in fancy dress. Battered furry top hats, waistcoats and trousers of a strange hard heavy cloth, with a fine odd pattern in the weave. The trousers tucked into riding boots with turned-over tops, and long heavy black whips trailing from their hands. The Bishop revised his opinion of them.

Not yobs in such elegant fancy dress. Street theatre perhaps? Students on a rag?

The Bishop wasn't the only one who had heard these disturbers of the peace. A buxom young waitress, with high colour, had issued forth from the brightly lit kitchen area, asking crossly what they were collecting for.

Her query turned into a shriek, as the first man picked her up bodily, whirled her round and round and deposited her heavily on the bar top. The Bishop pursed his lips, thinking that the spirit of student rags excused too much bad behaviour these days. Then he took himself sternly to task; it was harmless fun. The young were just different these days. He must not let himself become a fuddy-duddy at the age of forty-eight!

But however he tried, he could not persuade himself to approve of these goings-on. They were being much too familiar with the young waitress; not just chucking her under the chin, but in more embarrassing places. The girl was blushing furiously, positively wriggling with shame and embarrassment. The Bishop half rose to his feet to intervene, and then hovered despairingly. If he interfered, he would stand for the church being killjoy *again!*

He peered at the group, over the gold rims of his spectacles. He could not quite make out what was going on, from the back of the crowd. They were demanding something; but their voices were so coarse and loutish and uncouth that even he, a London churchman all his life, who could tell the dialect of Bermondsey from Hackney could not understand what they were shouting. They seemed to be saying they were coachmen, and that as this was the coachman's steakhouse, they were entitled to steaks for nothing. It really did seem in terribly bad taste – quite nasty and threatening. But then he often found Rags and street theatre threatening, under the thin mask of 'fun'. 'Fun' let strange things loose . . .

Now the girl's frightened yelling had brought out the manager; a big beefy man who carried a lot of authority behind a dinner jacket and a bulging paunch. The Bishop sat down again, relieved. No need for him to interfere now . . .

But the manager let himself be panicked. He began pushing the first of the dressed-up figures back violently, shouting. You could tell there was going to be trouble . . .

Above the top hats, the heavy loaded butt-end of a whip flashed in the dim light. There was a nasty scrunching thump, the crowd parted, and the manager staggered through holding both hands to his face, with blood spurting between his fingers. From the noises he was making, the Bishop could tell he was badly hurt . . .

He was faced with a choice. To get the man to medical care or to summon help. And the only phone was on the counter, beyond the crowd . . .

He held up the bleeding man, and glared back at the crowd, who were glaring at him in the most bestial, threatening way. But then he thought they noticed his clerical collar and purple front, and gave back a little. For once, he was grateful for his garb. He hustled the bleeding manager out to his car; perhaps there would be a phone along the way, from which he could call for help . . .

He thought he would drive the man straight to Casualty at St Winifred's Hospital. He could phone the police from there, too. But easier said than done; he found himself hopelessly locked into the evening rush hour. But he wasn't a London churchman for nothing; he knew every sidestreet. He swung left down Selby Road, towards the gaunt Gothic bulk of St Augustine's Social Club. A place of evil reputation; in the Bishop's opinion, a haunt of vice. Thank God it was the Pope of Rome who was responsible for it. It had become a place of bingo, of lotteries, of heavy drinking. It featured weekly in the court reports of the local paper. It made a lot of money for the local Church of Rome, but it had to employ bouncers and chuckers-out. All men of good Catholic families, it was boasted; all good churchgoers. Then two of those good Catholic churchgoers got done for inflicting grievous bodily harm and were sent down for ten months each . . .

In the dusk, the Social Club was lit up; great glowing lancet windows, and the nasty blue neon sign over the door. And the first huddle of the night's heavy drinkers ambling up to that door. Sickening.

And then, as the Bishop neared, he saw one of the heavy drinkers fall to his knees. Seven o'clock in the evening, and already paralytic. Then another went onto his knees; and another . . .

As the Bishop's car reached the entrance, he was slowed by traffic ahead. He had time to glance curiously at the little huddle of kneeling men. And what stood above them on the entrance steps.

A man in monkish garb, with arms upraised in . . . blessing . . . supplication? A man with a shaven tonsure that glowed pale in the ghastly blue light of the neons; sandals on his feet that were held on by no more than a strap round the big toe. It was the big toes that the Bishop remembered afterwards, in the flickering blue light. And the man's face under the tonsure; wild yet holy with blue wide-spaced eyes. An inspired face, a preaching face, a face calling for repentance. And apparently getting it, as more and more men below dropped to their knees.

It almost seemed, surmised the Bishop wildly, as if St Augustine himself had returned to earth and claimed the Social Club as his own . . . Then he took himself in hand firmly, and guessed it must be a bit of street theatre got up by Father O'Higgins of St Augustine's Roman Catholic Church. Very advanced theologically was Father O'Higgins. Very with-it. Just the kind of thing he would do in the middle of Lent . . . Well, the Bishop hoped it would work for him.

He snatched a gap in the traffic flow that a double-decker bus might have baulked at, tore round the big roundabout, and on to the forecourt of St Winifred's Hospital. He pulled up outside Casualty, and helped the injured manager out. The man would not take his hands away from his face – the blood still dripped through his fingers – and the Bishop did not feel like encouraging him to do so. Certainly his nose was broken, if not worse. He hurried him up the steps into Casualty, dreading what he might find. Friday night in the East End was starting early. There would certainly be fighting drunks inside; probably men with wounds from knife fights who would be so far gone they would mistake the nurses and ambulance men for their enemies and lash out with whatever came to hand. It took a strong stomach to work at St Winifred's Casualty . . .

But tonight, there was an unearthly peace; a too peaceful peace. The nurses and ambulance men stood around looking pale and shell-shocked. The Bishop led the manager up to a sister who looked like a zombie; who just kept on murmuring:

'She healed him. She *healed him.* She just laid her hands on his head and *healed him!*'

'Who?' said the Bishop, stupidly.

The sister turned to him with a beautiful, beatific dazed smile.

'Why, St Winifred, of course. She's come. She's taken over her hospital . . .'

'Where is she?' blurted the Bishop.

'Upstairs. In the wards. She's going from bed to bed, healing everybody. They're all asking for their clothes and getting us to book them taxis to go home. There's nothing else left for us to do . . .'

The Bishop looked at her hard. He had seen this state before. The sister was either suffering from advanced schizophrenia, or the kind of religious mania that Charismatics went in for. On the whole, the Bishop prefered schizophrenia. You could stabilize that with the proper drugs.

He turned to flee. Schizophrenic sisters and the intense silence of Casualty were unnerving.

The sister put a hand on his arm, and gave him a holy blissful beam.

'Stay, Bishop, and she'll heal you too!'

The Bishop fled. He could face drunks, wife-beaters, even murderers. But rampant religiosity . . .

When he got back to St Matthew's Vicarage, where he lived, the phone was ringing in the darkened hall. He picked it up with dread. He really didn't feel he could take any more . . .

It was Madeleine Trikes, of St Catherine's Nursing Home. A horrible private place that charged two hundred and fifty pounds a week. A gracious Regency mini-stately home in its own grounds, full of antique furniture, where you had to be careful where you sat, because the old people were not taken to the toilet often enough. A place where they sat in hopeless, pointless boredom, day after day. A place to reassure the relatives that they were doing their duty by their old people by means of beautiful oil paintings on the wall . . .

Madeleine Trikes SRN was hysterical. She was screaming at such a pitch the Bishop couldn't make out all she was saying. But it seemed this woman in strange garb had appeared, and said that *she* was St Catherine, and this was her nursing home, and she would do what she liked with it. And she was leading the old people in hymn-singing and they were making far too much noise, far too late at night. And she was threatening to sell all the antiques and spend the money taking the old people on outings . . .

'She's part of your damned religion,' screamed Madeleine Trikes. '*You* come and deal with her.'

The Bishop took the coward's way out.

'Why don't you call the police,' he said, and hung up.

He managed to pour himself a whisky with trembling fingers, and sat in the dark thinking wilder and wilder thoughts.

Had the Rule of the Saints come? Was this the Kingdom of Heaven come upon us? Had coachmen really reclaimed the Coachman's Steakhouse? Would St Catherine, having sold up the antiques in St Catherine's Nursing Home, go on to sell up St Catherine's Dock? Was St Peter already plundering the seat of the Pope in Rome, with a flock of rapacious and wealthy Italian antique dealers in his wake, raising the money from the sale of gold-casketed relics, the gilded baldichino and the old master paintings to feed the starving of Ethiopia? Flogging off St Peter's itself, Michelangelo's masterpiece, as a piece of first-class real estate on a prime city-centre site, to make sure that no child in the world was ever again hungry or abused? Would St Matthew turn up and claim this very vicarage, and the chair the Bishop was sitting in? Was the Devil himself sitting on Devil's Bridge in North Wales at this very moment, holding up the traffic with a grisly hand and charging tolls?

How would the world survive? Was this truly the Second Coming, that all those foolish Jehovah's Witnesses had so long looked for? Were the dead arising? Was Lloyd sitting once more in his bank, the rotting winding sheet still round him, and crumbs of grave soil dropping on the managing director's carpet? Was Barclay issuing cash to his old customers?

The phone roused him from his reverie at last. With shaking hands he lifted it, fearing the worst.

It was a minor canon of St Paul's Cathedral. Who couldn't raise the Archbishop. So would the Suffragan Bishop come and cope with the stocky, be-toga'd bearded man in the pulpit?

'He came in in the middle of a memorial service for Sir Hugh Willoughby, the critic. He's been preaching four hours already, and there's no stopping him. He's like a dam bursting. We've had the bit about all being members of the one body, and that bit about the superfluity of naughtiness, and he's describing the Damascus Road experience for the fourth time. They're all sitting there, just paralysed . . .'

The car journey seemed to take no time at all, through the darkened streets. There didn't seem any traffic about. Perhaps God himself was broadcasting on the nine o'clock television news . . . The great west doors of St Paul's were wide open, and light and the sound of a great impassioned voice issued forth. The Bishop was no longer afraid. He walked steadily up the central aisle, his feet echoing on the black and white marble tiles. Rank upon rank they sat, those who had four hours earlier come to pay a last tribute to Sir Hugh Willoughby, critic. The men in their pin-stripes, with neatly rolled umbrellas, the ladies in their discreet Anglican hats. Rigid as statues.

By and large, what the Bishop felt was a great relief. He knew he had not been a very good man; but he could not feel he had been very evil either.

Mainly, he had just been busy; or tired. Or both. He felt very tired now. Above all, he was glad to be laying his burden down, when he had braced himself, if need be, to carry it for another twenty-two lonely years.

He approached the well-known pulpit; he approached the well-loved altar. He had been a canon here himself, for many years. How nice to end, on your feet, with all your faculties intact, inside the masterpiece by Sir Christopher Wren, which was the building you loved best in the world . . .

But he was so tired. Too tired to hear what St Paul was saying properly. It seemed to be something about the need to wake up . . .

'Wake up, sir. Please won't you wake up. People are starting to come in for their steaks . . .'

A gentle hand was shaking his shoulder.

He opened his eyes and saw a white tablecloth, and a half-full cup of coffee.

He looked up at the rosy concerned face of the little waitress.

'I'm sorry,' he said to her. 'I seem to have fallen asleep. Sorry to have embarrassed you.'

'That's all right, sir,' she said, compassionately. 'You probably needed it. You're set up for the evening now.'

He got up stiffly, and left the Coachman's Steakhouse. The fat manager, face quite unmarred, gave him a sympathetic nod as he passed.

At the door, he saw it had started to rain.

He still had his meeting about one-parent families to go to.

Aunt Florrie

I've been helping my dad write Christmas cards. He
has such lovely ones. Blonde female Santas in mini-
skirts. Ones with reindeer so drunk they can't pull the
sleigh. My father is an Importer of Novelties. Our
house is lovely, too, at the moment. Ten-foot tree;
holly and ivy and mistletoe everywhere, and they're
all plastic. My mum is ever so happy there are no
needles and bits to Hoover up.

Anyway, there sits my dad, crossing people off his
Christmas-card list because they didn't send him one
last year, or they've gone bankrupt or something. But
he *has* got a heart.

'I'm wondering whether to send one to Old Charlie
Harris,' he says out loud. 'I've not seen him since we
left school in 1970, but he never forgets to send me
one, especially since I got a bit famous. Can't be much
fun for Charlie, enduring life in Liverpool Eight, with
six kids and no job. Don't know how he can afford to
send cards, on the dole. But I'll not consign him to
oblivion. Not for the price of a twenty-pence card
and a nineteen-pence stamp. It's probably all he gets
for Christmas.' And he pulls the smallest of his cards
towards him, the one with the smudge on the back,

and sits with his pen poised, wondering what to say that will cheer up Charlie.

'At least you won't have to send one to Aunt Florrie,' I said to him. 'Now that she's dead and safely buried.' I said it with great Christmas thankfulness. You see, our family is not exactly a close one; we don't get together much, even at Christmas. There are Difficulties. I mean, my uncle Sammy is loaded, but he's a bookmaker, and not quite nice, and his wife is Catholic and pious and talks about Baby Jesus in the most embarrassing way, just when everybody's getting sloshed and having a really good time. And Uncle Henry is a Methodist and doesn't hold with drinking at all. And Uncle Tommy has got an embarrassing car with rust around the bottom that would look just awful parked outside the house; one of the neighbours might complain about it to the Council and have it towed away. And Aunt Cissie lives in Bootle, and the rest are just . . . well . . . poor. So we never saw anyone over Christmas.

Except Aunt Florrie, who'd invited herself to our house for Christmas Day every year for forty years. It started with my dead-soft departed grandparents, who never had the guts to tell her she wasn't wanted.

Aunt Florrie always arrived early, and her mouth was going full out even before you opened the front door to her. Probably telling the plants in the front garden to stand up straight and stop slouching because the weather wasn't all *that* cold. She would look at my father with her cold green fishy eyes, give him a whiff of her breath, which always smelt of fish too, and tell him his front path needed weeding. Then she would step inside and just stand, laden with her handbag and her umbrella and what she called her bits and pieces, until everybody ran to take things off her and help her off with her hat and coat. And she would tell whoever went to hang up her coat to fetch a hanger, otherwise they would give the coat a nasty, unsightly bump on the shoulders.

Then she would spread herself on the three-seater finest-English-leather Chesterfield in the lounge so that nobody else would be able to sit there for the whole of Christmas Day, and me and Stan, my brother, would have to sit on hard chairs brought from the dining room. Honestly, I don't know how she managed to fill that settee, even allowing for her massive pear-shaped body with her huge grey-clad thighs under a skirt that was constantly riding up to show off more than it should. From which all our family averted their eyes like it was the End of the World or some other Cosmic Disaster.

I used to wonder desperately if any male, even in the deepest depths of past time, had ever enjoyed looking up Aunt Florrie's skirt. But she has her son, Albert, to prove it, so somebody must once have done it.

Anyway, she would fill the rest of the settee with her handbag and her bits and pieces; the amorphous bundle of grey knitting that she never worked on and that never seemed actually to grow into anything from one Christmas to the next; and a huge crumpled paper bag of mints, which she chewed continuously when we weren't giving her something else to chew, and which frequently spilled its contents all over the floor, rolling into the far corners of the room, and which she expected us all to rush to pick up at least twice an hour. Then there were her holiday photographs from Benidorm the previous summer (or was it the summer before that? They always seemed the same to me; she always went to Benidorm and photo-graphed the same fat friends in front of the same pointless objects). These she insisted on passing around like holy relics during the exciting bits of *The Poseidon Adventure*, and wasn't satisfied till we'd made some comment like 'That's a lovely drainpipe', which I swear I once heard my father say.

She talked non-stop, even during the Queen's Speech, when she said things like 'I think she's put on weight this year' or 'She sits behind the desk to hide her varicose veins, poor thing.'

Her voice could drown the telly even when it was turned up full, the way Maria Callas could drown the chorus at La Scala in Milan. And there was no escaping into other rooms to watch the telly, even for Stan and me. (We have tellies in every room and a videotape machine in most, except the bathrooms, where my father says it would be dangerous.) No, she would come rooting us out if we were gone for more than three minutes, saying Christmas was the time when the whole family should be together. Once our Stan even dragged a portable into the downstairs loo, and she was hammering on the door of that, and he was shouting back that he had bad constipation, and she began threatening him with senna pods . . .

At the dinner table she always had three helpings of everything, helping herself with a little smile and simper so as not to bother anybody, even before anybody else had been offered seconds. The only time she stopped chewing was to adjust her false teeth with three loud clicks, or to say things to my mother like 'I see you've bought a smaller turkey this year' or 'Is this a Sainsbury's pudding? I've never liked Sainsbury's puddings.'

By midnight on Christmas Day, when she would finally go, my father would be sloshed to the gills and my mother spacing out intermittently. So that when Aunt Florrie said, with her fiendish grin, 'See you again next year!' they were only able to grin back and nod weakly. And thank the Lord for the other three hundred and sixty four Florrie-less days of the year . . .

So you can imagine our feelings when, a week before Christmas two years ago, Aunt Florrie was terminated by a double-decker bus while coming out of Lime Street Station without looking. My father said he never went to a funeral more gladly in his whole life. He even paid twice what he meant to for a wreath; out of sheer relief that she was at last underground and a real Christmas could begin, the first in forty years.

Mind you, it was a quiet Christmas, that one. Just the family: Mam, Dad, Stan and me. Dad had left it too late to invite anyone else around to share our post-Florrie paradise. But it was like the Kingdom of Heaven, even if our Stan was sick through gobbling too many liqueur choccies.

The next year (last year, that is) my dad was on the verge of inviting all and sundry, when a Christmas card arrived. A small, mean envelope of thin, grey, hairy paper that stood out among all the posh ones he got from his business associates, each trying to outdo the others with huge all-shiny-red cards with gold holly, or all-gold cards that played 'Jingle Bells' when you opened them, or comic ones of Santa going down the crematorium chimney by mistake.

As I said, a small, mean envelope. The kind Aunt Florrie used to send, I was thinking, when we looked down and saw the handwriting.

It was Aunt Florrie's writing. There was no mistaking that small, vicious, spidery script. The best forger in the world would rather try a Bank of England fiver than Aunt Florrie's handwriting. Inimitable.

With trembling fingers, my father opened it. It was indeed signed 'Love from Aunt Florrie' and even had three horrid little *x*'s. And in the corner it said 'See you as usual on Christmas Day.'

The postmark was two days before.

'There must be some mistake,' said my mother in a voice that suggested that the greenhouse effect was knocking on our front door at the very moment.

Dad ran out of the front door with the card and envelope into his Jag and was gone for three hours.

When he came back, he said, 'It's no forgery. The police got their handwriting expert on to it. He compared it with those letters of complaint she was always writing to them, about dog dirt in Lime Street. They'd never got around to clearing them out of their files. And the bloke said the ink was pretty new too.'

You may wonder why the police were so helpful. All I can say is that, as an Importer of Novelties, my father is in a position to do the police a few favours, like providing plastic decorations for the Police Ball and other Deserving Charities.

Then my father added, 'I've talked to the post office too. They're sure it was posted within the last two days.' He'd done favours there too, you see.

As my father said, that Christmas card had all the awful certainty of a letter from the Inland Revenue. We all were quite horribly afraid Aunt Florrie was on her way again.

'But how?' asked my poor father. 'I saw her put six foot under. I even lingered to watch the gravediggers shovelling back the earth on top.'

'They buried the wrong person,' said my mother, trying to convince herself. 'A mix-up at the mortuary. I'll bet that son of hers, Albert, was just a big enough twit to keep his eyes shut while he was identifying her corpse.'

'It can't have been a lovely sight, at the best of times,' said my father. 'And after a double-decker bus . . .'

'But where's she been, all this last year? She let Albert sell up her house and furniture and didn't stop him. And that's not like Florrie . . .'

'Amnesia,' announced our Stan, who watches far too many horror videos in the middle of the night when my parents are asleep and they think he is too. 'She lost her memory and wanders abroad, a dark, sinister figure in the shadows . . .'

'If she's lost her memory,' said my father, 'how come she's remembered about coming here for Christmas Day?'

'She is being drawn by dark forces beyond her control,' said Stan.

'I'll give you dark forces,' said my mother. 'Here you are at twelve o'clock still not washed and dressed, and running around wrapped in your quilt like the Sheikh of Araby. You must've been watching telly since five this morning.' Little did she know he'd been up all night.

'All right, then,' said our Stan viciously. 'She's not lost her memory. She was properly buried, with you watching. So what does that make her? One of the Undead, sitting up waiting in the family vault at the cathedral cemetery.'

'You mean, she's sitting there writing Christmas cards and waiting to nip out to the post once the sun, which is death to all vampires, sets over the horizon of Liverpool Eight?'

I think my father meant to be sarcastic, get a laugh. In which case he failed. Nobody laughed. Our whole family's so hooked on horror videos, we know more vampires than people. I think they weaken your brain, horror videos.

My mother said, with a nervous giggle, 'Well, if she did suck our blood, she'd only complain about the quality of it.' If that was meant to be a joke, that didn't work either.

We didn't do anything else about it, because there was nothing else to do. Except my father didn't invite anybody else around for Christmas Day, just in case.

On Christmas Eve our Stan said, 'Don't worry, Dad. She'll have to come in the dark. She'll either be here before seven o'clock in the morning or we'll be OK till teatime.'

On that cheering thought we went to bed. But not, for a long time, to sleep. Not me anyway. I heard a dragging sound coming upstairs at half past two and nearly buried my head under my quilt, awaiting the horrid fangs in my neck. But then I heard a young voice say, 'Oh, heck', in a most un-Aunt Florrie sort of way. It was Stan, dragging what looked like a small tree upstairs.

'What on earth . . .?'

'I'm going to cut ash stakes from it. To hammer through her heart.'

'What a pity,' I said. 'It's still got oak galls sticking to it.'

I came awake with a horrid jump at half past seven, surprised to find I was still alive. I looked in the mirror, holding my neck to search for fang holes. But there was only the fading love bite that Angela Strang gave me at the third-year party at school, and her intentions were entirely different.

Then I whipped downstairs to the kitchen to make sure Aunt Florrie wasn't sitting there, spilling crumbs of soil all over the new cushion-vinyl and chewing at our cat's neck for starters.

There was no sign of her; just an endless trail of torn Christmas wrapping paper and crumbs all around the house as our Stan raped and pillaged his Christmas presents and helped himself to dates from the lounge and sausage rolls from the kitchen fridge at the same time.

He gave me an evil grin, full of sausage-roll crumbs and date.

'He's come!' he said, only his mouth was so chock-a-block with sausage roll and date, it came out mushy.

'She's *come*?'

'I said, "He's come." Santa!'

'I wish you wouldn't speak with your mouth full!'

'We'll be all right till four o'clock now. The sun's shining. Nice bright day. Not a cloud in sight!'

But we did not have a merry day. I couldn't bring myself to care if this year the *Poseidon* sank with all her passengers aboard or not. The Queen's Speech meant as much to me as a goldfish mouthing in a bowl. Stan kept on and on about how she would come.

'Mebbe, quietly, just as a bat, flying through the window like in *Grandson of Nosferatu*. Or mebbe with a chainsaw in both hands, like in *Dracula's Chainsaw Massacre*.'

My mother got up and closed the top window-light, which she'd just opened to let out the near-Russian industrial pollution of my father's chain-smoking.

'That'll not keep her out,' said Stan with satisfaction. 'Once a vampire's been asked in by somebody in the house, they get in anyway. As a cloud of mist. And we asked her often enough, for Christmas dinner.'

The trouble was, she was so much *there* already. The Christmas decorations, the balloons and snow-sprinkled Bambis hanging on the wall, just sort of conjured her up. And I wouldn't have sat on that three-seater all-English-leather Chesterfield to save my life. There was a deep depression in one end, worn there by her huge bottom on successive Christmases. I sort of couldn't sit there out of respect for the dead. Or pure panic.

My mother drew the curtains long before daylight faded. But it wasn't cosy. It just meant we couldn't see her coming. And I kept remembering her sitting there from other Christmases, eating her way through boxes of figs, Turkish Delight ... It would take more than figs and Turkish Delight to satisfy her appetite now.

'I wonder if she *will* fly, like Dracula,' said Stan. 'If so, she ought to be here any minute. But she might have to walk – there aren't many buses running on Christmas Day – and I bet the undertaker didn't leave any loose change in her pockets ... It could take her hours yet if she has to walk.'

'Would you like a nice, quick, clean death instead, our Stan?' said my father. 'Like me strangling you with a nice, clean bit of plastic clothesline?'

But nobody laughed. Even Stan stopped gorging himself on the handmade chocolates. There was a marvellous smell starting to come from the kitchen: roast turkey, roast potatoes, stuffing. It just made me feel sick.

At twenty past four exactly, at the end of twenty minutes of sweating silence and the sound of my belly rumbling, there came a hammering on our door knocker.

'She's made good time if she's had to walk,' said our Stan.

My dad just sat there paralysed, puffing on his forty-second ciggy of the day.

'Shall I let her in, Dad?' asked Stan. 'After all, it is Christmas.'

My father tried to answer the door with my mam's crucifix in one hand and her jar of dried garlic from Sainsbury's in the other. He found it quite hard to open the door with his hands full, and shaking, and sweating. I kept on thinking she'd made a pretty horrible human being, she'd make a truly appalling vampire.

He got the door open at last. The first thing I noticed was that there was more than one of them, a lot more. I thought wildly that she must have brought some mates from the crypt.

For the creature in the front had her face ... her green, fishy eyes and stinking fishy breath. Only thinner ... and all the hair was gone from the top of the head. At least a few straggly strands of hair had been combed across to hide where the skull shone through. And all the little creatures around had her face as well.

And the front figure was wearing feller's trousers and shoes. I thought wildly, a vampire in drag is too much.

I think I screamed before I realized I was going to scream.

'Merry Christmas, Frank,' said the creature in a timid, non-vampire voice, grinning. 'Don't you recognize me?'

It was her son, Albert. And all his family.

'Come in,' my father said. Then he fainted.

*

'It were like this,' said Albert, sitting on the all-English-leather three-seater Chesterfield, with all his family. With a double whisky in one hand and one of my father's best cigars in the other. 'It were like this. After the funeral we had to clear out her house. And we found all her Christmas cards still on the hall table, stamped and ready for posting.

'And our Chrissie here said, "Waste not, want not", and brought them home so she could cut off the stamps and reuse them. Only them only being seventeen-p stamps, we couldn't reuse them till this Christmas, for our own cards. Anyway we'd done our cards one night last week, and it was getting late, so she left our cards on the hall table, with me mother's cards on top, ready to cut the stamps off the next day.

'But silly, bloody little Herbert here thought he'd try and be helpful and took the whole lot down to the postbox at the end of the road and posted them. He can't read yet, you see. He's only seven.'

Herbert grinned at me, as if he was really proud of what he'd done.

'Well,' continued Albert, 'by the time we'd battered out of him what he'd done, it was too late to do anything about it. The last post had gone. So we thought the best thing we could do was to spend Christmas Day going around to all the relations she'd written cards to, explaining what had happened, to put their minds at rest, like.

'And we've had such a day of it! Everyone was that pleased to see us and have it all explained to them. They've been generous, very generous. Sammy offered us all the drinks and mince pies we could sink, and then Henry gave us a really smashing lunch. (Henry has Christmas dinner at lunchtime, 'cause he has to preach somewhere afterward, being a lay preacher.) And then high tea early, at our Tommy's. We were received like the Prodigal Son – the fatted calf wasn't in it. Best Christmas we've had for ages, wi' me laid up wi' me back so much, so I can't work, and nothing for Christmas Day in our house . . .'

He sniffed at the smell coming from our kitchen, appreciatively. What could my dad do but invite them to stay for Christmas dinner? After they'd been so kind and self-sacrificing?

I can truly say they ate and drank us out of house and home. Dates, nuts, sherry trifle, Babychams, sparkling Asti Spumante, the lot. A proper horde of locusts couldn't have done better.

They didn't go till midnight, after the last bit of Turkish Delight had vanished. And two of the kids were sick on the new wood-block parquet flooring in our hall.

'Well,' said Albert between drunken hiccups, 'you've made us very welcome, Frank, very welcome indeed. Who would have thought it possible, after all those years of not seeing you.' Then he shook Dad's hand on the doorstep, and so did his thin wife, Chrissie, and little Michael and little Herbert, and little Yvonne and little Patrick, and little Olly and little Bernadette with the green icicles hanging off the end of her nose.

'Now that we've started again,' Albert added, 'we must keep it up. Blood's thicker than water, when all's said and done. See you again next Christmas!'

I don't know about the spirit of Christmas, but I knew then that the spirit of Aunt Florrie would live for ever.

As Stan said thoughtfully, 'There's more ways than one of being a vampire!'

And that's why, when I've finished helping Dad do his Christmas cards, our whole family is jetting off into the sun, to spend this whole festive season in New Zealand.

I mean, you can't get any farther away, can you?

The Beach

Alan remembered reading an old story once – perhaps by Erskine Childers – about the Germans invading England on an August Bank Holiday Monday. Because everything was shut down, and everyone flopped-out in a heatwave, the Germans had a walkover.

Their ideal landing beach, thought Alan bitterly, would have been Southwold, Suffolk. Where his family came every year for a holiday.

There was something terribly wrong with Southwold. Instead of arriving all weary, and leaving set up for the winter, you arrived all bouncy, full of ideas, and left feeling like death warmed up.

Every year they loaded up the Volvo for the Great Adventure, with tennis rackets, binoculars, Dad's latest model sailing boat, guidebooks to churches and pamphlets about what's-on-in-Suffolk.

And every year, by the end of a fortnight, Suffolk had defeated them.

Tennis was fun at first. Dad's great booming erratic service that hit the net with an impressive thwack more often than it went in. Mum luring Dad to the net, then lobbing him into screaming frustration. Even the fact that Anita gave a hideous shriek every time she missed, and fell on her bum every second time she hit the ball. Hilarious!

But nobody else ever came to that tennis club. Every time you paid the lady at number seven and got the keys, you found the same footprints on the gravel court that you'd left yesterday.

And no matter how fast Dad's new yacht sailed, there was nothing you could do with it but sail it from side to side of the yacht pond, and after an hour it was totally boring.

And after the second one, all the great Suffolk wool churches looked the same. They all had wonderful roofs, brasses to rub, alabaster monuments gathering dead flies.

And you could have enough of morris men, brass bands and village shows.

You always ended up doing the gift-and-card shops. When Mum started doing her cards and gathering her gifts, you might as well be back home already. Because you knew the Great Adventure wasn't going to happen again this year. And every heatwave morning, as the sun climbed, you felt wearier. And in the end you just dragged yourselves down to the beach hut, for the day.

That was the point when the sea mist always seemed to start. The sea had been quite exciting before that, because there was an oil rig on the horizon, and boats passing. Coasters going up to Yarmouth, and fishing smacks with strange registration letters, that might have belonged to Lowestoft, and mysterious grey ships that just might have been

Russian spy trawlers. And a yellow powerboat, vaulting across the waves. And Dad's binoculars were snatched from hand to hand, and violent arguments broke out, if only on the topic of was that or wasn't it a lesser black-backed gull.

But once the mist came down, there was nothing to see at all. Except mist. It seemed to hang about thirty yards offshore, like a grey theatre curtain that was never going to go up again. No matter how hot the day, the grey curtain hung there and, by three o'clock, your skin started getting damp with it. Alan grew furious that the sun didn't drive it away. But Mr Burleigh, the man who hired out deckchairs and was the sage everyone turned to when baffled, said that the sun *made* the mist. On cold days, the horizon was quite clear . . .

So there you sat, with the sea wall behind you, and the mist in front. What made it worse were the breakwaters that ran down the beach every thirty yards. They reduced the long sweep of beach to little separate rooms, with floors of sloping shingle. And the same people seemed to gather in the same room every day. Just sitting there, in long rows of deckchairs against the breakwaters. Gossiping, quarrelling, falling asleep, waking up to ask what about an ice cream or a cup of tea, or were there any sandwiches left? But mainly asleep; under newspapers, or with heads tilted on one side and their mouths open. For God's sake, why did they come here to *sleep* – when they could sleep at home for nothing? Didn't they know time was passing? That there was only a short run to Christmas and then it would be 1990 and they would be another year older, another year nearer to that old man in the end deckchair whose hands shook non-stop so that anything he did took ten minutes, even eating a sandwich?

Alan felt sometimes, especially towards the end of an afternoon, like suddenly leaping to his feet and shouting at them all, like an Old Testament prophet forecasting the end of the world.

But he didn't, of course. He would pad off in his striped orange-and-blue bathing trunks in search of the *real* instead.

Real inside the amusement arcade. Spotty youths shoving in money like there was no tomorrow, pulling the chrome handles without a clue, just to impress the stupid girls who hung on their elbows. If you watched any particular fruit machine long enough, you could guess when it was coming up to dropping a jackpot. Then you could drift up to the couple working it and stare rudely, till they got uncomfortable and moved on. Then, after three or four goes, you got the jackpot yourself; a shower of coins spilling over on to the dirty floor, among the flattened fag ends.

But it was a dark, miserable kind of reality, that made Alan feel dirty himself afterwards.

Better to stroll along the prom and watch the bodies of the girls, walking along in their bikinis. Brown and rounded, exciting. Like the bunches of grapes hanging among the boring dusty leaves of the vineyards in France. Single girls with fellers; bunches of girls laughing on their own.

He never tried to chat them up. He wasn't interested in their minds, which were just full of

giggles, or what Bet Lynch had said in the last episode
of the Street. Their minds were just an extension of
the Great Dreary Desert. But their bodies were a
promise of something better, that never seemed to
happen. Yet the promise was nearly as good as a feast.

Sometimes, up on the prom, he'd come across
newspaper placards, proof that there was life outside
Southwold. But even they seemed to shrink in scope
as the heatwave rolled on. From 'Gorbachev sacks
party bosses' and 'New threat by Ayatollah' to 'Out-
break of foot and mouth' and 'Bather drowned'.

His other great source of the real was the sea. Just
watching the waves break soothed him; letting his
mind fill with their roar and rattling ebb. Like the
beating of some gigantic heart. But the best was to
wade out into them till you were up to your neck,
giving little upward hops to keep your mouth clear of
the wave tops as they passed. Then to lie back and
let the waves lift you; feel each one as it coursed
through your body from your heels to your head.
Letting your flesh become part of the wave, letting
the sea have its way with you. Helpless. Very relaxing.
Sometimes he fell asleep, floating, and only wakened
when the waves had spun him round to face the sun,
and the sunbeams forced their way in through foam-
speckled eyelids.

He came back from one such trip to find his whole
family asleep. Mum looked pretty cool, with her
mouth shut and her big mirror sunglasses on, and
her neat plump body very brown with just a hint of

red in it, and the latest Iris Murdoch paperback *The Book and the Brotherhood* lying open face-down across her chest. Alan thought she looked so cool some passing bloke might have picked her up, if Dad hadn't been there.

But Dad was there, sprawled like a disaster area. Anita had piled sand all over him, and he hadn't even stirred. A hairy man was Dad; beard and hairy chest, all full of drying sand. Mouth open, snoring, and all his fillings showing. Make a good book jacket for a Stephen King chiller. The Southwold Horror.

Anita was asleep, face down in a sandy copy of *Jackie*. Open at the problem page, but the creeping sand was erasing the problems, as it had once erased the Pharaohs.

Them all being asleep made him feel desperately cut-off; as if they'd gone off into the land of dreams and left him abandoned for ever. He had a selfish panicky desire to shout or bump into their deckchairs, or trample on them by accident, just to wake them up, make sure they were really still there. But people got so mad with you, when you did that. So he just bent and looked at Mum's watch on her wrist. Only half past three. God, two hours before there was any chance of going back to the digs to get ready for supper. He lay down on the sand feeling quite hopeless. The people next door seemed to be asleep as well, but they'd left their tranny on. Broadcasting the Final Test; running down to a hopeless draw on a dying battery. The commentator was talking so slowly he sounded like he was falling asleep as well. Alan had a sudden feeling that the whole world was just running down, like a clockwork toy that God had forgotten to wind up. The world needed *energy* to drive it, and the heatwave had sucked all the energy away.

He squinted down the beach, with his right eye as it lay against the sand; making the nearby pebbles look as big as boulders on the moon.

That was when he noticed the girl walking towards him, the only thing moving on the whole beach. He noticed her first because she had a gap of nearly two inches between her thighs. Some girls, he'd noticed, had no gap at all between their thighs, so that their thighs rubbed together as they walked in their bikinis. Others had quite a large gap; full of bikini, of course. It wasn't that a gap turned him on or anything. It was just something you noticed, if you watched a lot of girls walking about in bikinis. A gap wasn't necessarily attractive or anything . . .

But this girl was attractive. She walked proudly, head held high like a queen. Her skin was very pale, hadn't been in the sun much yet. And her bikini was black. He watched her appreciatively as she approached. Then thought sadly that, in a minute, with a squeak and swish of dry sand, she'd be past, and he'd never see her again.

But she didn't swish sand over him. He had lowered his head out of politeness as she got very near, and now he saw her long slim white toes stop dead in front of him. In the end he looked up timidly, and she was looking down at him between the beautiful black cones of her bikini. She said:

'Hello. You look a bit lost.'

'I am.' He tried to give her a bold friendly grin, but it didn't come out right, because he was staring up at her at such an angle, and getting a crick in the back of his neck.

As if she'd read his thoughts, she sat down abruptly and arranged herself cross-legged, like a buddha. The position created all kinds of exciting folds of flesh. He didn't know where to look, so he sat up quickly himself. He glanced at his parents, to see if they were watching, fearing knowing grins on their faces, and a giggle and sarky remark from Anita. But they were all lying exactly as before. He felt ashamed of his father's gaping mouth. What would the girl think?

She followed the direction of his eyes. 'S'alright', she said. They won't wake up for a bit.' She sounded so sure of herself, he felt slightly annoyed. Then she said:

'You're Alan Dean, aren't you? I've got a message for you.'

'How'd you know my name?' He pretended outrage; but it is not unpleasing when a pretty stranger knows your name.

'That'd be telling,' she said. Oh, God, she was one of those. He hated girls who made mysteries. On the other hand, he liked girls with long black hair, wet from the sea, that sent runnels of moisture trickling down their cleavage and under their costumes.

She smiled at him and said:

'It's no good looking at me like that. I'm dead, you see.'

*

He gaped at her far too long. He was far too slow in saying, 'Oh, har har!' He wasn't at all sure he liked cocksure jokey girls like this one, who enjoyed saying crazy startling things. What she meant probably was that she didn't feel sexy; that being in the sea had made her cold and shrivelled up where it mattered. The sea did that to him, too; after a bathe, he became no bigger than a winkle.

'No, I don't *mean* that,' she said sharply. 'I mean I am really dead! I'm a ghost.'

'And I'm Batman. And Robin too, in my spare time.'

She laughed out loud at that. That pleased him. He liked making girls laugh; it gave him a sense of power. He did it a lot. It was safer than making a heavy pass at them.

Then she stopped laughing and said, 'I'm serious. I am a ghost. I got drowned swimming off Walberswick yesterday. I went out too far and the current carried me away and I couldn't get back. They found my body on Dunwich beach this morning. The tide carried it south. It always does.' She gestured vaguely southward.

That was her mistake. He made a sudden snatch, and grabbed her wrist.

It was, of course, absolutely solid; bone and sinew under soft attractive flesh.

Just cold, that was all. From being in the sea.

'Gotcha!' he said. 'You're as real and solid as I am.'

'Yes,' she said sadly. It really seemed to take her down a peg. She lowered her eyes, and looked at his hand holding her wrist. He was holding her tightly,

113

though not tight enough to really hurt. But his fingers dented her sleek skin. He liked that; again he felt a sense of power.

She just didn't seem to know what to do next. Then she said, conspiratorially, in a lowered voice, 'I really am a ghost, you know. Let go of me and I'll *show* you.'

The way she said 'show' excited him more. Maybe it was a memory of other girls who had shown him things when he was younger; long ago.

He glanced furtively at his family.

'I *told* you,' she said impatiently. 'Don't worry about them. They won't wake up for a bit yet. *Look!*'

She pulled her hand away, and gestured up towards her own face.

He looked at her face intently. She seemed to be making an inner effort of some sort; though it could simply have been an effort not to laugh. The distant Southwold pier, with its few and dreaming fishermen, seemed to run in one of her ears and out the other; it would have made a very comical photograph . . .

She went on making her effort; he went on staring at her intently; he wasn't going to grumble about that. She had a face well worth staring at. Her high rounded forehead looked even higher, with her long hair pulled back by its own wetness. Wide apart eyes. When she grew up, she would look a bit like Anna Ford. The only thing that spoilt her face were the little bits of thin green seaweed. One piece came down out of her hair, and hung a little way down her rounded forehead. The other piece seemed to have stuck to the corner of her mouth. She didn't seem to know it was there. He wanted to reach out and take it off gently, but he couldn't quite pluck up the courage.

'Well?' she asked expectantly.

'Well what?'

'Can you still see my face?'

'Course I can see your bloody face.' Then he was sorry, that he'd said 'bloody'. She had a very beautiful face.

'Ooooooh,' she said, in girlish exasperation, and took a deep breath, which suddenly made her bikini exciting. 'I'll try one last time.'

And this time her face went ... slightly blurred. Enough to make him raise his hand and rub his own eyes. He'd been staring at her too intently, too long, that was all.

But when he opened his eyes again, she had grown more blurred, even misty.

'Damn,' he said. Rubbing your eyes sometimes made them worse, particularly on the beach, when salt and sand got on your lashes. He rubbed harder, and looked again.

There was a fisherman walking along Southwold pier now. And at the point where that fisherman should have vanished behind her head ...

He stayed in sight. He walked right across her face and out the other side, and stood on the end of the pier, looking at the sea and lighting the tiny dot of his pipe.

'Yewhat?' He went on staring stupidly at the distant fisherman. As if the fault lay in *him*. Then he came back to his senses, and switched his eyes back to her face.

Which was as solid and beautiful as it had ever been.

'That was a *trick*,' he said.

'I'll have to practise,' she said. 'It's harder with you, because you're . . .'

'I'm *what*?'

'I mustn't tell you yet . . .'

Oh, God, she was back to her stupid teasing ways again. Girls in this mood were bloody exasperating.

And yet some little doubt remained. It had been a strange trick she had pulled; making her own face as transparent as glass. It had left him feeling quite odd and lost. He reached out and grabbed her hand again. Partly to reassure himself; partly because he liked doing it.

And of course, her hand was as solid as before. He could feel the slim elegant shape of her fingerbones through her soft flesh.

But she was so *cold*. Her cold seemed to run right up his own arm. It wasn't just the cold of somebody who's been swimming; he'd been swimming himself.

It was the cold of a vase full of water, on an icy winter's day.

The sea couldn't be that cold. This was August, in the middle of a heatwave. But as he went on holding her hand, the cold worked further and further through him.

In the end he had to let go of her. He was panting; panting with *cold*.

'I *told* you,' she said. 'I'm cold because I'm dead.'

'Bollocks. You're not dead.' He used it as an excuse

to examine her in every detail. The soft shine of the skin on her young shoulders; her breasts in the bikini, like little apples; the soft small roundness of her belly, with its perfect little navel . . .

'Why don't you look at my feet,' she asked. She lifted a slim white foot and waved it at him.

'What's wrong with your feet?'

'No sand on them. I've been walking with wet feet on dry sand, but there's no sand on them. Everybody else has sand on theirs. Even if they haven't been swimming.'

He looked back to the safety of his family. Sleeping Dad had caked sand on the soles of his big sprawling feet. So had sleeping Anita. Even sleeping Mum had a bit. Then he looked at his own.

'I haven't got any sand on my feet.'

'No,' she said, so sadly it terrified him, he didn't know why. He didn't dare to ask why.

'Look,' he shouted. 'You feel solid to me, so you can't be a ghost. I *felt* you. And you're walking and talking, so you can't be dead.'

Then he realized he was screaming at the top of his voice. He looked round, embarrassed, to see who he'd wakened up; who was staring at him with sleepy accusing eyes.

Nobody. The sleepers slept on as before. He might as well have never shouted. For all the effect he had had, he might as well not *exist*.

But he did exist; like the girl existed.

'Look,' he said. 'Have a biscuit, have a Kit-Kat. My mum's got some in her bag. That'll prove you're alive.'

He still thought up till that point that he was talking to a girl who was potty. Beautiful and friendly but quite potty. The only real worry he had, as he reached for Mum's big fashionable straw basket, made in Italy, was that the Kit-Kats would be sticky – melting with the heat.

His hand seemed to miss the bag. He wasn't looking what he was doing; he was still looking at the girl. He turned his head with a grunt of exasperation, and grabbed the handle of Mum's bag properly.

The handle seemed to run through his fingers like the dry sand of the beach. Like it was thinner than the dry sand of the beach. Like it was the air itself.

He couldn't believe his eyes; he couldn't believe his hand. He grabbed and grabbed and the bag never moved. It might as well have been a hologram of a bag.

In total panic, he turned and grabbed the girl's hands again.

'But *you're* solid!'

'Because I'm dead and you're dead. How could I eat your silly Kit-Kat when I'm dead?' And she opened her pretty lips wide.

And her mouth was full of weed and sand.

'But *I'm* not dead!' he cried out.

'You were doing your floating act,' she said, 'and you drifted too far out. That yellow powerboat ran you down. They were going so fast, they didn't even notice. Nobody knows you're dead yet. That's why. I was sent to tell you . . .'

'Rubbish,' he shouted. '*Rubbish!* I'm alive, I tell you. *Alive!*'

'All right,' she said, gesturing at his family. 'Tell them you're alive. Tell everybody. See where it gets you. I tried to break it to you the easy way. But I don't suppose there is any easy way. You have to find out for yourself.'

He ran and ran. He ran everywhere about the little town of Southwold. Up the little sleepy Georgian main street, through the lazy shoppers; into the church, to try to make the vicar understand; but the vicar was too busy to notice, talking to the ladies who were polishing the brass and arranging flowers. Up to the lighthouse and the green where the old cannons still stood. Then back to the beach.

In time to see them bringing a body ashore; a body silent and floppy and naked, save for blue and orange swimming trunks.

His swimming trunks.

'C'mon,' said a voice at his elbow. 'It's not so bad once you get used to it. But it's funny how you ran about everywhere, just like me. I suppose everybody runs about everywhere, trying to prove they're not dead. And you suddenly find when it's too late that you love everything you thought you hated, don't you?'

She took his hand, and it was so *cold*. The cold in her started to seethe and bubble all over his body.

He suddenly shouted at her, in a rage:

'If I'm dead, why'm I not as cold as you?'

He squeezed her hand harder and harder, as if to

show his rage with all the world. And her hand crushed and oozed into a freezing pulp.

He heard his mother's voice say sharply:

'Oh, Anita, what a *stupid* thing to do! Look at the mess you've made!'

And Anita say, whingeing. 'It was Alan made the mess, not me. It was only a *joke*.'

'Waste of a good ice cream,' said Dad crossly. 'Fancy dropping it in his hand like that. Couldn't you see he was asleep?'

'I just thought it would wake him up. I didn't know he was going to *squash* it.'

Alan felt his left hand not just freezing, but sticky. He opened his eyes and the setting sun shone straight into them. He raised the hand to block out the sun's rays, and freezing drops fell on his chest. Blearily, he saw he was clutching a misshapen red and silver paper, from which white and brown liquid dripped. A drop fell in his mouth and tasted sweet.

'Give me that hand,' said Mum, grabbing it and extracting the silver paper, and wiping his fingers with the wet facecloth she always carried to the beach. 'Anita, you are the *end*.'

It had all been a dream. He had fallen asleep, sprawling, mouth wide open. Just like Dad.

The girl had just been a dream, he thought again. The yellow powerboat roared past once more, was, for a moment, faintly visible through the mist, then vanished into obscurity.

Only a horrible dream.

The Beach

At least he thought so, till they climbed the long steps back into the town, and he saw her photograph under the screaming headlines of the local paper.

Daddy-Long-Legs

Granda's house was much too close to Hitler.

The only people in Garmouth who lived closer than us were the lighthouse-keepers on the end of the piers. All there was between us and Hitler was the North Sea. On sunny evenings I used to watch the little white fat clouds blowing eastward, and think that by morning they would be looking down on places in Norway and Denmark and Holland where grey soldiers strutted around doing the goose-step in their jackboots, and people crept about in fear of a hand on their shoulder. I even worried about the clouds a bit.

We were on a tiny headland that jutted out into the mouth of the Tyne. Not worth defending, the soldiers from the Castle said, as they laid their long corkscrews of barbed wire inland from us. There was a checkpoint a hundred yards away up the pier road, where sometimes, with bayonets fixed to the rifles on their shoulders, they demanded to see our identity cards. But usually they let us through with a wink and a thumbs-up, because they knew us.

The Old Coastguard House, they called my grandfather's house. It was really only a white-painted cottage, with a little tower one storey higher than the roof. The tower had great windows, watching the Tyne on the right, the bay of Prior's Haven on the left, and the Castle beyond, and the North Sea in front. My granda had stuck great criss-crosses of sticky tape over the windows, to save us being cut to bits by flying glass if a bomb fell near. He had scrounged a lot of sandbags from the soldiers, in exchange for the odd bottle of my grandmother's elderberry wine. The soldiers were very keen on my grandmother's elderberry. They said a nip of it was as good as a tot of whisky when you were freezing on guard duty of a winter's night. My granda filled the sandbags with soil from the garden, leaving a great hole which filled with water when it rained in winter. My grandfather considered keeping ducks on it, but he thought the firing of the Castle guns would scare them witless during air raids, and besides, the pond dried out completely in summer. A pity, because the ducks' eggs would have helped the war effort.

My grandfather built up the sandbags round the windows of the cottage, till we looked a real fortress. Of course he couldn't sandbag the tower windows, they were too high up. But nobody was supposed to go up there during air raids.

I think people worried about us, stuck out there on our little headland. They offered us an Anderson air raid shelter for the garden; but Granda said he preferred our cellar, which had walls three feet thick. They offered to evacuate us altogether. But Granda said he wasn't going to run away from bloody Hitler, into some council house. He would face Hitler where he stood; and he ran up the Union Jack on our flag-pole every morning to prove it. He and I did it together, standing to attention, then we saluted the flag and Granda said, 'God save the King', without fail. Grandma said we should take it down during air raids, as it would make us a target. Granda just made a noise of contempt, deep in his throat. Otherwise, though, Grandma was as keen on the war effort as we were, collecting in the National Savings every Tuesday morning, knitting comforts for the troops, keeping eggs fresh in isinglass, and bottling all the fruit she could lay her hands on.

I remember I'd just got home from school that December night. The cottage looked dark and lonely, and my guts scrunched up a bit, as they always did when I passed the checkpoint and said ta-ta to the soldiers, who always called me 'Sunny Jim'. Granda would still be at work down the fish quay, and Grandma would be finishing her shopping up in Shields. There would be a lot to do: the blackout curtains to draw, the lamps to light (for we had no electricity) and the ready-laid fire to set a match to. Grandma had left some old potatoes in a bowl of water, which meant she wanted me to peel them for supper and put the peelings in the swill bucket for Mason's pig . . .

I had just lit the last lamp, in the kitchen, and was rolling up my sleeves to tackle the potatoes, when I saw the daddy-long-legs come cruising across the room. It was a big one, a whopper. It looked nearly as big as a German bomber, and I hated it as much. I mean, I love bees and ladybirds, but daddy-long-legs hang about you and suddenly scrape against your bare skin with their scratchy, traily legs. Given half a chance they get down the back of your neck. It was long past the season for them, but this one must have been hibernating or something, and been awakened by a sudden warmth. I backed off and grabbed an old copy of Granda's *Daily Express* and prepared to swat it. But it had no interest in me. It made straight for the oil lamp, and banged against the glass shade with that awful persistent pinging. And then suddenly it went down inside, between the shade and the glass chimney. I could still hear it pinging and see its shadow, magnified on the frosted glass. God, it must be getting pretty hot down there . . .

I squinted down cautiously between the shade and the hot chimney. It was hurling itself against the chimney, mad to reach the flame. Silly thing, it would do itself an injury . . . Then I noticed that one of its long crooked legs had already fallen off. As I watched, another broke off. But still the creature hurled itself against the chimney. Another leg went, then another, and there was a stink of burning that was not paraffin. Then it fell against the chimney with a sharp sizzle and lay still at last, just a little dirty mark. There was a tiny wisp of smoke; the stink was awful.

Feeling a bit sick, because it had been a living thing, I went back to peeling the potatoes.

It was then that the siren went. I ran to the door, slipped through the blackout curtain and went outside to look for Granda and Grandma. It was quite dark by that time; but I heard a distant tiny fizz, and the first searchlight came on at the Castle. A dim, poor yellow beam at first, but quickly followed by a brilliant white beam, so bright it looked nearly solid. High up, little wisps of cloud trailed through the beam, like cigarette smoke. Then another beam and another. Four, five, six, all swinging out to seawards, groping for Jerry like the fingers of a robot's hand. Then more, dimmer, searchlights, up towards Blyth. And more still, across the river in South Shields. It made me proud; we were ready for them, waiting.

But in the deep blue reflected light, which lit up the pier road like moonlight, there was no sign of Granda or Grandma. I could see the two sentries on the checkpoint, huddling behind their sandbags, the ends of their fags like little red pinpoints. They'd be in trouble for that, if this raid was more than a false alarm. You can see a fag end from five thousand feet up, my Granda says...

But otherwise, the pier road was empty. And there was no chance of them coming now; the wardens would force them down some shelter, until the raid was over. I was on my own. I felt a silly impulse to run up and join the sentries, but they'd only send me back into cover. And besides, it was time to be brave. I checked the stirrup pump with its red buckets of water, in case they dropped incendiaries. Then I did what I was supposed to do, and went down the cellar to shelter.

But there was nothing to do down there. By the light of the oil lamp, trembling slightly in my hand because it was so heavy, all I could see was Granda's three sacks of spare potatoes, and the dusty rows of Grandma's bottles of elderberry. This year's still had little Christmas balloons, yellow, red and blue, fastened over their necks. They were still fermenting. Some of the balloons were small but fat and shiny; others looked all shrivelled and shrunken.

I should sit down on a mattress and be good. But it was cold and I couldn't hear anything. I mean, the Jerries might be overhead; they might have dropped incendiaries by this time, the cottage roof might be burning, and how would I know? When he was there, in an air raid, Granda kept nipping upstairs for a look-see. As the person in charge of the cottage tonight, so should I. Or so I told myself.

I crept upstairs. Nothing was on fire. Everything was silent, except for some frantic dog barking on and on, up the town.

And then I heard it; very faint, far out over the sea. *Vroomah, vroomah, vroomah*. Jerry was coming. You could always tell Jerry, because the Raff planes made a steady drone. But Jerry's engines weren't synchronized, Granda said.

And as I went on listening, I knew there was more than one of them. The whole sea was full of their echoes. My stomach drew itself up like a fist. I wasn't scared; just ready. Your stomach always does that.

Then the whole blue scene turned bright pale yellow. The earth shook, and the universe seemed to crack apart like an egg. The Castle guns had fired. I waited, counted under my breath. Seventeen, eighteen, nineteen. Four brilliant stars out to sea burnt black holes in my eyes. They were in a W-shape, and everywhere I looked now there were four black dots in a W-shape. Then the sound of explosions, rolling in across the water like waves. Then the echoes going away down the coast, off every cliff, fainter and fainter.

The guns fired again. People were rude about those guns. They said they never hit anything; that they couldn't hit a barn door at ten yards. That the gunners should get their eyes checked. But, tonight ... There was suddenly a light out to sea, high in the air. A little yellow light where no light should be. The Jerries never showed a light, any more than we did.

But this light grew. And now it was falling, falling. Like a shooting star, when we say that it is the soul of someone dying.

And I knew what it was. We'd hit one. It was going to crash. I leapt up and down in tremendous glee.

Burn, bastard, burn. We'd had too many folk killed in raids for us to love the Jerries any more.

It never reached the sea. There was such a flash as made the guns look like a piddling Guy Fawkes' night and a bang that hurt my ears. But I could still hear faint cheering – from the Castle, from across the river; very faint, in South Shields. Then there was just a shower of red fragments, falling to the water.

But the rest of the planes came on. The guns went on firing. They were nearly overhead now. There was a faint whispering in the air, then a rattle on the pantiles of Granda's house above me. I ducked down into the cellar entrance. It seemed especially silly to be killed by falling *British* shrapnel ...

I didn't poke my head out again until it was quiet. Far up the river, the bangs were still lighting up the sky. The red lines of pom-pom tracers climbed so slowly, so lazily. Then the whooshing flicker of the Home Guard's rocket batteries. And the tremor of the first bombs coming, through the soles of my shoes. It was Newcastle that was copping it tonight . . . we could do with a break.

It was so peaceful, to seawards. Just the faint blue light from the searchlights, which could have been moonlight . . .

And then, by that light, I saw it. White, like a slowly drifting mushroom.

A Jerry parachute. I could see the little black dot of the man, under his harness. He was going to land in the water of the harbour; he was going to get very wet, and that would cool his courage, as Grandma always said. He might drown . . .

The parachute collapsed slowly into the water about two or three hundred yards out. Ah well, they'd pick him up. The picket boat on the defence boom that lay right across the river. It would be full of armed sailors. I was just an interested spectator.

But for some reason, the picket boat continued to stay moored to the far end of the boom. There was no sound from its heavy diesel engine. Come on, come on! The bloke might drown . . . Or he might come ashore and do anything. Myself, I hoped he drowned.

But I watched and watched, and that boat never stirred. Maybe they hadn't noticed the parachute; maybe they'd been following the raid up the river, like I'd just been doing . . . Maybe the Jerry wasn't drowning; maybe he was swimming ashore at this very moment.

And we were the nearest bit of shore.

I decided to run for the sentries. But at that
moment, a second wave of bombers droned in. The
shellbursts overhead were churning the sky into a
deafening porridge of flashes. I could hear the
shrapnel falling, rattling on the roof again. I daren't
go out. I'd seen what shrapnel had done to one of
Granda's rabbits, old Chinnie. I had found her. The
roof of her hutch was smashed in, and the floor, and
Chinnie lay like a bloody cushion, blue Chinchilla
fur hammered into the ground in a mass of wooden
splinters and fluff . . .

I hovered piteously from foot to foot. Oh, please
God, send him to land somewhere else. South Shields,
the rocks below the Castle . . .

I thought at first it was a seal in the water. We get
the odd seal up the Gar; they come in for the guts
from the fish-gutting, when they're really hungry –
even though the Gar is an oily, stinking old river.
Sometimes they bob around out there and stare at
the land, the water shining on their sleek dark heads.

But seals don't have a pale white blob where their
face should be. And seals don't rise up out of the
water till their shoulders are showing, then their whole
bodies, the gap between their legs. They don't haul
themselves out of the water and begin to climb the
low soily cliff.

Oh, God, let the guns stop, let the shrapnel stop!
But a third wave was vrooming in overhead, and a
piece of shrapnel suddenly smashed our front gate
into a shower of white fragments.

Suddenly, I made up my mind that I would rather
be smashed to a bloody pulp by British shrapnel

than be in the power of the Swastika. Holding my arms above my head in an absolutely hopeless attempt to protect myself, I ran for the smashed gate.

As I went through it, a very big, very strong hand grabbed me. I think I squealed like a shot rabbit my father had once had to kill with a blow to the back of the neck. I think I kicked out and bucked wildly, just like that very rabbit, fighting for its life. My efforts were equally useless. The huge hand carried me back to the front door and flung me inside. Our little hall was filled with a huge gasping and panting. Our front door slammed shut. The hand picked me up again and carried me into the living room and threw me on a couch. And for the first time, I saw him.

He was huge, black, shining and dripping water all over Grandma's carpet. He trailed tentacles from his body with little shining metal bits on the end. And he did look like a seal, with the leather helmet almost crushing his head in so that only his eyes showed, and his pale long nose, and his mouth, gaping like a fish's.

'Others?' he shouted. 'Others?' He stared around him wildly, then seemed to remember something suddenly and felt, groped at, his shining, dripping side. And pulled out something black with a long tube . . .

I recognized it from the war magazine that my father used to buy me, before he joined the Raff. It was a Luger automatic pistol, with a twelve-shot magazine. All the Jerry aircrew carried them.

He tore off his leather helmet as if it suddenly hurt him. It made him look a bit more human; he had fair hair, quite long, a bit like our Raff types, which surprised me. Funny how you can still be surprised,

131

even when you're almost wetting yourself with terror . . .

'Others?' he said a third time. He was listening. It made him look like a wild animal, alert. Then I twigged what he was getting at. Was anybody else in the house? Then he grabbed me again, shouting, '*Raus, raus*!' and dragged me from room to room by my hair.

When we had searched everywhere, even the lookout tower and the cellar, he brought me back and threw me on the couch again. He listened to the outside; the raid had quietened. But he was still shaking. Then he fell into Granda's chair, and we stared at each other. I didn't much like the look of him at all. He had green eyes, too close together. My Granda always says never to trust a man who has eyes too close together.

Then he pointed the gun at me (I think he enjoyed pointing the gun at me) and said, 'Food!'

What could I do but lead him to Grandma's larder? And get him our only half-loaf from the enamel bread bin. And the butter dish from the top shelf, with our tiny ration of butter and marge, mixed together so it would last longer. I began to cut a thin slice, but he pushed me aside into a corner with the gun-barrel, then put the gun down and smeared the whole half-loaf with all the butter and marge and began to wolf it down, tearing off huge chunks. I noticed he had very large white teeth, a bit like tombstones. When he had gulped it all down, he poked me into the larder with the gun again, and went along the shelves to see what else he could find. He found our little cheese ration and swallowed it in one mouthful, just tearing off the greaseproof paper with his large teeth, and swallowing so fast you could tell from the gulp he gave that it hurt him. He found a quarter-jar of jam and began to eat it with a spoon, his gun in his left hand now. Then three shrivelled apples, which he stuffed into a pocket of his dripping suit. Didn't they feed them, before they came on a raid? Were all the Germans starving, like our propaganda used to say, back in the phoney war?

How did I feel? I felt the end of the world had come, the worst had happened. That I, alone, in Garmouth, was already under the Nazi jackboot. That I was now already inside the Third Reich. He might do anything to me . . .

And yet nothing was changed; the fire still burned on steadily, making steam rise from his suit, as he sat by it. There were Granda's old pipes in their rack, and a twist of tobacco in its silver paper. There was Grandma's knitting still in her chair. The world had turned insane.

And then I began to worry about Granda and Gran. Soon, the raid would be over. Soon they would come walking down the pier road, and straight into . . . Granda might try and do something; he was as brave as a lion. The German would shoot him. Then he might shoot Gran too . . . But what could I do? Nothing. Even when the noise of the raid stopped, there was no point in shouting. The sentries on the checkpoint would never hear me. And then he would shoot *me* . . .

He was watching me now.

133

'Derink!' he said. 'Derink. Derink!' He made a drinking motion with his free hand.

Like a slave, I crept into the kitchen. A slave of the Third Reich. I got our half-bottle of milk from the cooler on the floor, put it on the kitchen table, and turned to get the tea and sugar canisters and the teapot . . .

'Derink!' he shouted again, and swept them all off on to the floor in his rage. The milk bottle broke and the milk and fragments went every where. 'Derink!' He raised his hand to his lips again, and threw his head back. I could tell from the shape his fingers made, that he meant he wanted a bottle. He pointed down the cellar. '*Wein . . . vin . . . wine!*'

He must have noticed the row of bottles, Gran's elderberry, when he searched the cellar. I took up the oil lamp and went down for some. He didn't follow me; only stood by the cellar door, listening to the outside.

The long rows of bottles glistened in the lamplight. They were arranged by year. Gran kept her elderberry a long time . . .

And then it came to me. Gran's elderberry . . . people laughed at it because it wasn't proper wine. But it was strong stuff. She gave the curate from the church a glass of her old batch once, and he liked it so much he'd accepted a second . . .

He was so drunk by the time he reached Front Street that he fell off his bicycle. Elderberry gets stronger every year you keep it. This year's – 1940 – still fermenting, wouldn't do him any harm. But

1939 . . . 1938 . . . I picked up two bottles of her 1938, dusted them with my hand, and carried them upstairs.

He gave a quick, wolfish grin. '*Wein? Ja! Ja!*' He couldn't get a bottle open quick enough. Pulled the cork out with his strong tombstone teeth and spat it out, so it bounced on the hearthrug. Then he raised the bottle, threw back his head and the sound of glugging filled the room. It was already much more than the curate ever had.

He stopped at last to draw breath. His wolfish grin was wider.

'*Wein. Ja. Gut!*' He seemed to relax as it hit him. Stretched his legs out to the fire. Then he had a long think and said, quite clearly but slowly, '*Engländer* not our natural enemy are!' He seemed quite pleased with himself. Then he took another swig and announced, '*Engländer* little *Brüders* . . . broth . . . brothers are.' He put down the bottle for a moment, and reached out and patted me on the shoulder. Then he picked up the bottle again and offered it to me, indicating that I drink too.

I made a right mess of it. I didn't want to drink, get drunk, and yet I had to. Otherwise he might suspect I was trying to poison him . . .

So I drank, and it went down the wrong way, and I sprayed it all over the place and went into a helpless fit of coughing.

He threw back his head and laughed as if he thought that was hilarious.

'*Wein* . . . not . . . little *Brüders ist*. Big men . . . *Wein*.' He drank some more. The bottle was half empty by now. The more he got, the more he seemed to want. And, oddly, the better it made his English.

'English little *Brüders* . . . but Europe is corrupt . . . we must make a new order . . . then . . . happy!'

I just waited patiently. Time was on my side now.

It began to have an effect on him. He began to slump deeper into his chair. But the hand with the gun kept playing with it twitchily. I was dead scared it might go off. And he wasn't grinning any more. He looked at me solemnly, owlishly.

'*Prost* . . . drink toast. To Rudi! *Mein Kamerad!*' More wine glugged down, while I waited. Then he said, in a small hopeless voice, 'Rudi *ist tot* . . . dead. *Und* Karli, *und* Maxi, *und* Heini. *Alles* . . . *tot.*'

And then, unbelieving, I saw a tear run down his face. Then another and another. He put his face in his hands and sobbed like a woman, only worse, because women know how to cry properly. He was just a gulping, sniffing, revolting mess. I reckoned that any minute I'd be able to snatch the gun from where it lay. But I didn't know how to use it . . .

'*Kamerad, Kamerad,*' he moaned; comrades, comrades. He was rocking in his chair, like a woman rocking a baby.

And I just waited. Then he began to sing, like a lot of drunks do. Something about '*Ich habe einen Kamerad*'. It was horrible. It embarrassed me so much my toes squirmed inside my shoes.

But I went on waiting.

Finally he stopped, a stupid look of alarm growing on his face. He tried to get up and failed, falling back heavily into the chair. He tried again, pressing down with his hands on the chair arms. And since he had the bottle in one hand, and the gun in the other, he didn't make it again. The hand holding the bottle opened, and the bottle fell to the rug with a dull clunk and rolled towards me, spilling out a trail of dark elderberry.

Slowly, at last, like a very old man, he managed to lever himself to his feet, and stood swaying above me. I thought he was going to shoot me then. But he decided not to; perhaps he remembered he had sent me for the wine – his little slave labourer.

Instead, he made a wavering track for the door, crashing into every bit of furniture on the way, hurting himself and gasping. Suddenly he reminded me of something. And I remembered what it was. The daddy-long-legs, in the oil lamp. Like it, he had come flying in; like it, he was dashing himself to bits. I almost laughed out loud. Except that pistol was wavering all over the room.

Then it suddenly went off. Even in the middle of that raid, the noise was deafening. A panel of the door suddenly wasn't there, and the air was full of a Guy Fawkes smell, and the smell of splintered wood. That piny, resinous smell.

Then the gun went off again. He cried out, and I saw blood pouring from a tear in the leg of his wetsuit. And then, with a wild yell, he was out of the front door and the wind was blowing in.

I think I ran across to replace, of all things, the blackout curtain. We were trained so hard to keep the blackout; it was second nature. But as soon as my hand was on it, I heard a yell and a big splash from outside. I knew what had happened. He had fallen into our sandbag hole – the hole we had thought of using for a duckpond.

I ran to see. He was just a series of sodden humps, face down in the water. He didn't move at all. Suddenly a mass of bubbles rose and burst where his face would be, under the water. It was unbelievable. I mean, that hole was only about seven feet across. There wasn't a foot of water in it.

And yet I knew he was drowning. As I watched, one hand came up out of the water and clawed at the side. But it couldn't get a grip, because the sides were steep and slippery. His head turned, his face looked at me and then fell back, and more bubbles came from his mouth.

Soon, any minute now, he would move for the last time; then he would be dead. One dead murderer; one dead Nazi thug.

What made me jump into the hole beside him? Try to lift him out and fail, for he was far too heavy for my eleven years? What made me force my legs under his head and lift his face clear of the filthy, muddy water, so that he could groan and choke and breathe and mutter to himself in a language I would never understand. '*Freund, Freund*!' His big hand wandered round my body, till I grabbed it and held on to it.

'*Freund, Freund.*'

And that was how we stayed, while the returning bombers droned back over us, and the guns fired intermittently, and the shrapnel sang its awful song to earth.

And that was how Granda and Gran found us, and stared at my mudstained face, after the all-clear had gone. By the light of the fires from the burning docks at Newcastle.

'God love the bairn,' said my gran. 'What's he doin' wi' that feller?'

Granda took a careful look. 'Reckon that feller's a Jerry. Run for the sentries up at the wire, Martha.'

I had nothing to say. I was so cold I could not move my jaws any more. But I kept wondering why I did what I did. He was a murderer. Maybe he was the pilot who dropped the bomb that killed my mother at Newcastle, when she'd just nipped down to the shops for a box of matches to light our fire.

That's when my dad joined the Raff. To get revenge on the bastards who killed my mother.

So why couldn't I just let him lie there and die? I thought a lot about that. It wasn't because he'd ever been nice or likeable; it wasn't even because he'd cried for his dead mates. It wasn't even because if I'd let him die, *I* would have killed him. It was a heroic thing to kill a Nazi in those days. Everyone would have thought me a hero.

No, it was just that he was still alive. And I didn't want him dead in Granda's garden. I mean, if he'd died, he'd still be there, to me. Even if Granda filled the duckpond in; which he did, a few days later, shovelling soil from all over the garden into it, furiously. Saying it was a danger in the blackout.

His name was Konrad Huess. I know because he wrote to me after the war, to thank me. Sent me lots of photos of his wife and kids. I was glad, then. For his wife and kids. But I never replied. I was too mixed up.

I still am.

The Trap

I can't speak of the way Stephanie Harcourt died.

You probably read about it in the papers; I couldn't bear to. She was my neighbour and my friend. And I saw the face of the man who found her dead, and I'll never forget it.

I hadn't seen her for about three days. She often popped in for a coffee, mid-morning. Or around teatime, with a few cakes she'd baked. Or I'd see her round the shops, or out mowing her lawn. She kept busy, because her husband was out in Saudi Arabia. She'd tried living out there with him, but she couldn't take the heat and the boredom. She said she couldn't live without green grass, and the smell of rain. She was a passionate gardener; my garden is still full of the cuttings she gave me. It's all I have to remember her by. I miss her, being a widow, with children far away. She was ten years younger than me, thirty-five.

I don't know why I didn't miss her sooner. But I was so taken up with my cat, William, who was also missing. And she was always popping off to see her parents in Birmingham, because of being alone so much. Her father had an electronics firm there, very hush-hush. Though she once mentioned computers and artificial intelligence, and another time she said they were working on a new lie detector for the FBI. The firm must have been doing very well, the presents he was always giving her. Not just hi-fi stuff, like Bang and Olufsen, but marvellous intricate old clocks, antiques that must have cost a fortune. She was an only child. She seemed very fond of her parents.

The first hint of trouble was Tom, our milkman. He knocked on my door, because two days' milk had piled up on her step. Tom takes his duties seriously, with people who live alone. He saved the life of one old woman down the village, who was lying helpless after a stroke. And Tom was a worrier.

I'm afraid I pooh-poohed him, rather. Stephanie was always the picture of health. She swam, and played tennis twice a week. And we weren't a worrying sort of district; a large village full of big old houses, and no council estates full of the unemployed within ten miles. People were still a bit sloppy about locking their doors, then. We didn't even have a Neighbourhood Watch Scheme.

I told Tom not to worry; she must have forgotten to cancel the milk. I even asked him to keep an eye open for William. Then I went and collected the milk off Stephanie's doorstep. It was a beautiful morning in June, and her lawn was just beginning to re-sprout daisies. Somehow, that convinced me she must be away; she was very regular with the lawnmower. I remember how nice the sun looked on her front door. There was no hint of what lay behind it. The first day's milk had gone off, pushing the cap up with a column of clogged sour cream. But the second day's was usable. I hate waste.

As I was picking up the bottles, my cat William came strolling home, looking as pleased as Punch with himself.

That was the last good news I had for a long time.

The next thing was a ring on my front doorbell. Ring, ring, ring. I stamped down the front hall calling, 'All right, all right. Where's the fire?'

I opened the door, and a very young policeman was standing there. Swaying. Holding himself up with one hand on my ornamental urn. His face was so white that his freckles stood out like bloodspots. He was staring at something over my left shoulder. He moved his lips and nothing came out. I helped him into my lounge, thinking he'd been taken ill. He fell into my sofa, then suddenly bent over and was sick all over my Persian rug.

I still couldn't get any sense out of him. He just went on staring and shivering. So I reached for my cordless phone, and dialled 999 and reported a policeman in distress. Even then, I was ironically amused. The rug was probably ruined, but insured. I was already shaping the whole thing into an amusing story for the tennis club . . .

Half an hour later, an inspector came round to put me in the picture. A much older man. I would have said a hardened man except that his mouth, too, had fits of trembling as he spoke.

The young policeman had been our new beat

constable. Keen to make good. Tom the milkman had met him on his rounds, and mentioned the bottles of milk. Having nothing better to do, he'd decided to check up. Knocked on the front door, then gone round to the back. Found it swinging. Walked in and found . . .

It was only by the grace of God it wasn't me that found her. I'd meant to nip round the previous night, only I'd spent too long looking for William instead. Me worried about William while Stephanie lay . . .

It was the way she must have had to suffer. In silence, with that ragged chewed bloody gag in her mouth. All those hours, with only a brick wall between her and me. With the soothing sounds of the village coming in to her ears. Mr Jenkins cutting his hedge, lawnmowers, the fish man slamming his van doors.

As the Inspector got up to go, I asked whether I'd be able to see her, later, at the Chapel of Rest, to say goodbye. The Inspector tightened his lips and shook his head silently. Nobody would ever see her again, except the one who identified her and the forensic experts. Somehow, that made her doubly lost. I kept seeing her face, smiling at me. Her hands delving lovingly into the earth of her garden.

I cried a long time. Before I realized that the murderers might have come to my house instead.

They never caught anybody for it. There were bloody handprints on the wallpaper, but they didn't match anything in the police records. A lot of her nice things were taken, small antiques and jewellery. But they never turned up anywhere. That was the worst thing, in a way. That they'd been cool enough to walk off with her things, after what they'd done to her.

I don't know how I lived through the next two weeks, next to that empty house. Like everybody else in the village, I invested a fortune in locks and bolts. One day I counted four vans from home-security firms in our road alone. Down in the village, husbands were actually nailing up back doors and screwing thick plywood over back windows. Half the women were on the verge of a nervous breakdown. There was wild talk of enrolling wives in the local pistol club. One farmer's wife nearly blew off her own husband's head with a shotgun. Only her hands were shaking so badly she blew a great hole in the ceiling instead.

It was impossible to sleep, until dawn and the first passing traffic. You can fit the best locks and bolts in the world, and in the middle of the night they seem no better than bits of wet paper. And all day the phone ringing. Women friends and neighbours. 'Are you all right? Are you all right?' But every time the phone rang, you thought something else terrible must have happened.

In the end, after I had watched Stephanie's husband go out through the front gate with the police, I took myself and William off to my daughter's in Portsmouth for a while. I never saw a man with a face so ruined. I knew he'd never get over it. He went off back to Saudi, to live as he could.

When I came back from Portsmouth, her house was up for sale. So were four other houses in our road. But there didn't seem to be any buyers. Or I'd have put my own on the market.

And Stephanie's garden, her lovely garden, went to rack and ruin. The grass of her lawn grew knee-high. The privet hedge grew like a forest, as if the house was crouching in terror behind it.

I think I might have gone out of my mind, for sheer lack of sleep. Until, one lunchtime, waking doped with sleeping pills, I looked out of my bedroom window and saw a furniture van standing at the gate of Stephanie's house. I thought at first they'd come to take the last of her furniture away. But no, they were carrying stuff in. And there was a stranger, a white-haired man in a suit, telling them where to put it.

That was the first time I saw Mr Megstone.

All I felt was rage, that anyone could be so inhuman as to want to live there.

Then I wondered if he'd come from a long way off, and didn't know what had happened in the house. Maybe the damned house agent had deceived him . . .

But surely he'd seen the blood splashes on the walls? The bloody fingerprints?

Maybe they'd redecorated . . . I struggled desperately with myself, to be fair to the white-haired man. After all, he looked old, and there was something rather frail in the way he moved.

I heard a gentle tapping on my front door, well before dusk. The westering September sun was still streaming through my lounge windows. So I went to my front door. Peeped through my new spyhole.

His face looked weird through the lens: all nose and mouth, and the eyes a long way back. But then everybody looks the same through a spyhole. You learn to make allowances. Otherwise I thought it was an impressive face. Very intelligent, but very tired. As if he'd lost nearly as many nights' sleep as I had. Not days' tired, but months' tired. As if he was driving himself just to keep going. Those deep determination marks round the mouth . . .

I hadn't the heart to insult him by opening the door on the chain. Heart in my mouth, I opened it fully. After he'd said who he was, and we'd shaken hands, I asked him in for a cup of tea. That was the funny thing about Mr Megstone. I liked him at first sight. Even now that I know the appalling things he did, even now I've seen the graves, I still think of him sadly.

But that was long afterwards. That day, we talked gently over a cup of tea. I kept having the odd feeling I'd met him somewhere before, that his face, some of his gestures, seemed familiar. I asked him whether he'd ever lived locally. He said no, he'd lived in the Midlands all his life. He'd just retired, and this seemed a nice part of the world. He was a widower, with no children, so he could please himself.

The big question kept coming up into my throat, like a lump of unswallowed food. I couldn't bear not to ask it. Finally I said, 'You know . . . what happened next door?'

He closed his eyes, as if a spear had gone straight through him. 'Yes,' he said. 'Poor soul. I hate to think how she must have suffered.' Then he said, very humbly and apologetically, 'The house ... was very cheap. And I had to have somewhere to live.'

'Yes,' I said gravely. Almost mimicking his slow gentle tone.

'It's not the house's fault,' he said. 'The house is not to blame. It must have been a lovely house, before it all happened. She had such ... lovely taste ... in wallpapers and curtains and carpets.'

I shuddered, thinking about the wallpaper in that bedroom.

'I'm keeping that room locked up,' he said. 'I use it to store things.'

I shuddered again. What a strange thing to do. Every time he went in, he would see the bloodstains. But he was running on, gently.

'The garden was lovely, too. I shall try to get her garden back as it was. I think she would've wanted that, don't you?'

It seemed to me then, for a second, that he spoke a little too familiarly of her, as if he, some time, had known her. Then the thought got lost, because I started to cry, remembering her in her garden. It seemed a lovely thing to want to do, restore her garden. I dried my eyes, after a moment, and said so.

'You must have been very fond of her,' he said. 'I think she was very fond of you.'

'How can you know that?' Again, suspicion twitched in me.

He gave his weary smile. 'Just guessing. Two nice women, living alone, next door to each other.'

It wasn't until long after he'd gone that I asked myself how he'd known I lived alone.

But as the days passed, my suspicions faded. He was an attractive man to talk to, over the garden fence. And I was grateful that, as I watched him slowly and painfully putting Stephanie's garden to rights, his stooping figure began to erase the memory of her stooping figure. In some ways, his slow stooping patience reminded me of her slow stooping patience. And when, in October, he offered me some geranium cuttings, I could have wept. Stephanie had always offered me cuttings then.

It baffled me, trying to guess how old he was. I had thought him nearing seventy when I first met him. But, moving around the garden, his body seemed younger than his face. He seemed to have lost a lot of weight recently. His frame was broad, though thin, and his clothes tended to hang on him, as if made for a bulkier man. But he moved as gracefully and loosely as a boy. Far from nearing seventy, I guessed he must be nearing sixty. Some hidden grief had lined his face, and made him hesitant. And nothing attracts a foolish unattached woman like a sense of hidden tragedies in a man. Especially a man with such a lively curious mind as Mr Megstone. Talking over the back fence, his mind was into everything, with the curiosity of a boy, and the sureness of a man who has once held power. I wondered what he'd been, because he was clever with his hands, too; he mended my misbehaving lawnmower, that I'd put in for repair four times in six months; and it has never misbehaved since.

I wondered why he'd retired early, and what from, but my careful questions got me nowhere. 'Trade,' he would say, 'vulgar trade. Factories, dividends, filthy lucre. Isn't this a lovely rose tree? I hate trimming them when they're still blooming . . .'

'That was her favourite,' I said suddenly, tears in my eyes.

'Yes,' he said gravely, as if he'd known her all her life.

When he gently asked me to tea, I took a deep breath and went. It wasn't quite as painful as I'd expected. He hadn't changed any of her decoration, and most of the curtains and carpets were the same. But she'd always kept them plain and simple, and now they were sort of . . . lost . . . behind all his own furniture. Beautiful furniture, pictures, all antiques and *what* antiques! There must've been hundreds of thousands of pounds worth. The sort of stuff you don't see nowadays, outside of stately homes.

'I hope you've got good burglar alarms,' I said. It started as a joke, till I remembered we'd all had our burglar alarms fitted since Stephanie died.

'No burglar alarms,' he said, almost gaily.

'But you've got good locks and window catches . . .'

'No,' he said, 'I'm too old for all this newfangled stuff. If burglars come, they'll get in anyway. They just do more damage getting in, that's all.'

'But suppose they do break in?'

'If they come, they come. All the stuff's insured. Have another sandwich!'

I looked at him curiously. I'd got to know him pretty well by that time. I confess, I was strangely attracted to him. In spite of his deep underlying sadness. Perhaps because of it. He had an air of someone going inevitably to his doom, and not really caring. Gay, almost, at times with a kind of gallows humour. But this wildness of talk about burglars . . . as if he would almost welcome them . . . it seemed very wrong. I did not want it. I wanted to turn his gallant autumn back into a brief spell of summer. Indian summer, anyway. He had told me, in a rare moment of confidence, that he was fifty-seven. I was forty-six by then. It didn't seem an unbridgeable gap. A few happy contented years, on the brink of eternity . . . Of course, now I shudder. But I didn't know *anything* then.

We changed the subject, to the American dollar crisis and my falling capital. He certainly didn't seem in the least interested in my money; but he gave me a few bits of shrewd financial advice that I was glad later that I'd followed.

As I left, I noticed a wall-clock in the hall. A small beautiful clock, all intricate fretting and two shining brass weights.

'How strange,' I said. 'That's just like the clock that Stephanie had, the one they stole . . . after . . .'

For once, he looked suddenly guilty. Was lost for words. But he came back smoothly, 'A Viennese regulator. Very fine clocks. They're getting rather rare in this country now . . .'

Two odd things happened, after that. The first was the van outside his door, marked:

NEWTON AND TONGS. BOILERMAKERS

From the van's interior, two men with aprons carried a series of heavy steel plates, with holes drilled in them at regular intervals. And when I say heavy, I mean heavy; the two men were staggering as they carried them. All that day, there came a sound of drilling and hammering inside his house. I thought he had taken my advice about burglars to heart very seriously indeed. But then the men and the van went away, and the next time he had me to tea, there was no sign of steel plates anywhere. I just supposed that somewhere hidden, he'd built himself a strongroom. But what good was a strongroom, with antiques on display all over the house, and the locks and bolts no better than before?

The other odd thing he did was to sell that Viennese regulator soon after. He advertised it in all the local papers, among the adverts for Victorian fireplaces and modern vinyl three-piece suites:

> ELDERLY COLLECTOR WISHES TO SELL
> FINE EARLY VIENNESE REGULATOR.
> £700 FOR QUICK SALE.
> APPLY MEGSTONE, ARLEY VILLA,
> RADDON GARDENS, SOUTHWICK.

The implications horrified me. I went round to see him in a rage, the newspaper still in my hand. And I was sharp with him.

'Are you *asking* for trouble? Letting all the local burglars know you've got that kind of stuff, and that you're elderly into the bargain? Are you asking to have your house done over? You haven't got a burglar

alarm, and not a decent lock in the place ... you
bloody old fool.' Then I burst into tears.

He listened to me in silence, then gave me a clean
and beautiful white handkerchief, to wipe my tears
away with. I looked up at him, very shyly, in the end.
His face was concerned for me, but inexpressibly sad.
And stern.

'My life is my own, Marjorie,' he said. 'I have grown
fond of you, and perhaps you have grown a little fond
of me. But that does not give you rights over my life.
I must do as I think best.'

I was put out. Badly put out. It was as if he'd
looked straight into my heart, and seen what was
there, and gently rejected it.

I blundered out of the room. Anything to get away
from those gentle understanding eyes. I was in such a
state that in the hall I opened the wrong door: the
door that led under the staircase.

'Not that way,' he said, very sharply. 'You don't
want to see my domestic squalor.' And led me to the
front door by the arm. And asked me whether I was
all right, before he let me go home.

At home, I flopped on to my couch as hopelessly
as the young constable had, all those weeks ago. But
I wasn't sick; with me it was just tears. It was only
after I had stopped crying that I began to wonder
about the sharp tone in his voice, as he had led me
away from that doorway under the stairs.

Somehow, the tone had been wrong. It was not a
tone of male embarrassment.

It had been a tone of fear.

*

As I said, he sold the clock. Two weeks later, he advertised and sold a fine bronze statue of Venus, for a thousand pounds. Then it was a pair of gilt candelabra. The local newspaper finally cottoned on to what was happening and sent a photographer and reporter to interview him, and report on his collection. It was featured in a double-page spread. Including the fact that he thought burglar alarms were not much use. Then he got featured in the county magazine ...

I tried several more times to reason with him. Without result. Finally, in despair, I called in Jim Connor, our local beat constable. Jim was the one who had found Stephanie. I gave him the mug of tea that no policeman in his right mind refuses, and studied him.

He had not yet got over finding her. His considerable boyish charm seemed to have gone for ever. He was paler than I remembered him, and his right eyelid flickered from time to time, in an uncontrollable tic. But he seemed to be coping. There was a new discipline about him; and a caring. He had worked very hard to reassure us, since the murder, especially those of us who were living alone. Everyone spoke very highly of him; we had grown close to him. I thought he would make an excellent superintendent one day, intelligent and wise. If his nerve held out long enough.

I told him of my worries for Mr Megstone. To my surprise, his face lightened.

'I think you're worrying unduly, Mrs Fletcher. Mr Megstone might seem frail, but I think he can handle himself.'

I said sharply that I thought he was being unduly optimistic.

He leaned forward and said, 'Can I tell you something in confidence?'

I said I thought I could be trusted.

He took another sip of tea and said, 'I was on the early shift, about a month ago, when I came across Mr Megstone standing at his gate. He had a lad with him, a big rough lad in torn jeans I didn't like the look of, at all. Except he stood beside Mr Megstone very humbly, with his head down. Mr Megstone said he had caught the lad trying to break into his house. He'd had a good talk with him, and the lad had seen the error of his ways. In fact the lad had confessed to several other burglaries he had done, and now he wanted to go to the police station and make a clean breast of everything.

'I looked at the lad, incredulous. But he just glanced up, in a flinching sort of way like he was terrified of me, and nodded without a word.

'So I said all right, I'd take him in. And did Mr Megstone want to charge him with breaking and entering as well? Mr Megstone just laughed and said, "Well, he found my back door open, and he hasn't taken anything or done any damage, so I'll let him off this once. He's in enough trouble without me. Aren't you, Ronnie?"

'And the lad just nodded, with his head down. So I took him in, and he sang like a canary. We cleared up quite a lot of burglaries . . . The lad just seemed brainwashed . . . Didn't give a bit of aggro.'

'That's all very well,' I said. 'But the next one mightn't be so soft . . .'

'It might surprise you to know, Mrs Fletcher, that it's not the first time it's happened. If Mr Megstone keeps it up, my arrest record will be so good they'll have to promote me to sergeant.'

'I don't believe it, Jim. It's against nature.'

'Oh, it's all true. Times, dates, modus operandi. We've recorded a lot of stuff. Super's very pleased.'

'I don't mean that. I mean . . . how is Mr Megstone doing it?'

Jim shrugged uncomfortably. 'Dunno. Maybe he's a retired preacher. Maybe he gives them religion.' He was trying to laugh it off.

'Poppycock,' I said.

'I never look a gift-horse in the mouth,' he said.

We parted; not in a very good temper with each other.

An unease grew between me and Mr Megstone; a constraint. We still spoke to each other over the garden fence. But without warmth. Still, I confess I continued to watch him, as he came and went, and worked in his garden. And I watched that house more closely than I've ever watched anything in my life. Maybe Mr Megstone did feel he had a holy mission to reform burglars. But his adverts in the paper began to have the nasty look of the outer filaments of a spider's web. They sickened me. Burglars are not animals, to be snared for a hobby.

Anyway, I noticed immediately when Mr Megstone

went missing. One fine morning, he was not out working in his garden. I shopped at my usual time, and did not see him going round the shops. Coming home, I tapped on his front door. *That* front door. It looked so very much as it had on the morning I collected Stephanie's milk from the step . . . There was a pint bottle on his step now.

No answer. I managed to get myself through lunchtime; telling myself he might have gone to Manchester for the day, and that I was not his keeper. But I tapped on his door again at two. Still no answer. And the milk was still there. I drove into Manchester myself, and did some pointless shopping, because I was quite unable to sit still.

I returned at dusk. There were no lights on in his house and the milk was *still* there. I was so terrified that I hadn't the courage to park my car in the garage round the back. I scarcely had the courage to let myself into my own house. I put on the light in the hall, and rang the police station. All the time imagining what might once again lie behind my wallpaper and that innocent brick wall.

I asked for Jim by name. He was, as luck would have it, on the beat that night. They asked if it was urgent, and I said no, lying in my teeth. It was just that I'd like a word with my friendly neighbourhood bobby. It's funny, no matter how terrified you are, you're still more terrified of being thought a fool by policemen.

They said they'd radio him and get him to call, as soon as was convenient.

I'm glad to say he was round in a remarkably short time. I think he knew something was up.

'Mr Megstone's . . . missing.'

'Since when?'

'I haven't seen him since yesterday teatime – he was working in his garden. I've been knocking on his door all day. He's not in. The milk's still there.'

He looked at me, exasperated on the surface; but there was fear underneath. 'That's ridiculous. He might have gone to Manchester and stayed on for the pictures. It's only half past seven now!'

'He's never away. I don't think he has anywhere he wants to go to. I see him every day. If he was going anywhere, he would've told me.' My voice rose to a wail. I knew I was sounding childish.

'Sorry. There's nothing I can do. There's nothing I can tell the duty inspector. I have no *grounds* . . .'

'Be damned to your grounds,' I said. 'If you don't *do* something, I won't stay in this house tonight. I'm taking William and going to my daughter's. And I'll be obliged if you'll wait and see me off the premises.'

He put on his be-reasonable act. 'I know what you've been through, Mrs Fletcher . . .'

'Then *do* something about it.'

He hesitated. Then grinned. A nice grin, but weary. 'I'll knock on his door. I'll check round the back. You'll have to be satisfied with that.'

It was a start. I locked up my house, leaving all the lights on, and we went.

No answer to his knock. Mr Megstone hadn't drawn his lounge curtains, and I could see the backs of his chairs, by the distant streetlight.

He knocked again, then said, 'OK, we'll try the back.'

And went off very quickly, shining his lamp here and there, over Stephanie's plants.

He stopped; said abruptly, 'The back door's open.' There was a slight tremor in his voice; he was remembering the other time.

My head spun, and I had to put one hand against the wall to stop myself falling.

'Now I've got grounds to enter.' The official heavy tone was back, but it couldn't quite hide the fear. 'Shall I take you home first?'

'No, I'll come with you.'

'Probably nothing. He probably went out and forgot to shut his back door.'

Neither of us believed him. I saw him reach inside and click the light switch. The light didn't come on. He turned his pale face to me, a blur in the gloom.

'Odd.' I saw his dim hand reach for the radio clipped to his tunic. But it fell away again. Like me, he was afraid, but more afraid of making a fool of himself, radioing in about nothing.

He made up his mind with an effort, and pushed on into the kitchen. Shone his torch around. Nothing but Mr Megstone's familiar kitchen things, kettle, mixer, two plates and a bag of flour on the red formica table top. With their shadows fleeing away behind them, strangely, in the light of the torch.

'Nothing here, then.' There was a slight catch of relief in his voice, like a death sentence postponed. He pushed the door open, into the hall.

There was a streak of light on the left. In all the darkness, just one streak of light.

'That's the door under the stairs,' I said.

The door Mr Megstone had got scared about when I went to open it.

'Be careful,' I said, pointlessly.

He swung that door open.

'Good God!' But it was incredulous relief in his voice, nothing worse. 'Look at this!' He plunged down inside.

I followed, and looked where he had gone.

A small room, dimly and goldenly lit. A chair on each side of the door: upright, ugly steel chairs, incredibly strong looking. But I hardly spared them a glance. For the whole far wall of the tiny room was a showcase. A glowing showcase full of the most magnificent jewellery display.

'Must be worth a fortune,' he said, breathless. Breathless with expecting a corpse, and finding a king's ransom.

I went to follow him; there were three steps down. But it wasn't the steps that made me hesitate; it was a dark two-inch groove across the threshold, under my feet, a seemingly bottomless groove . . .

I hesitated because I could not think what such a groove should be for. But I only hesitated for a moment, then I stepped down after him.

'One of these cabinet doors is open,' he said. And reached up to it; whether to close it or not I will never know.

For as he moved it, there was a downward move-

ment at my back; I felt the swift draught of its passing
before I heard that terrible clang.

I whirled round, and where the doorway had been
was a solid steel plate, thick with rust and grease.
Without hinge or handle. Now I knew what the groove
across the threshold had been for; and the boiler-
makers. A steel plate that had dropped like a
guillotine.

We were caught like rats in a steel trap.

For behind the innocent floral wallpaper the walls
were steel; and under the white vinyl paint, the ceiling
was steel; and under the soft thick green carpet, the
floor was solid concrete.

'Neat,' said Jim viciously, as he gave up lifting the
carpet and tearing off wallpaper, and probing the
ceiling with his clasp-knife. 'A rat trap for burglars.
And jewellery for bait. The old sod must be out of
his mind. He'll get two years for this. I'll have his guts
for garters . . .'

He clicked on his radio. His hand was trembling,
but his voice was steady, while he called the police
station.

Until the station didn't answer. Or rather, answered
with a blurred and useless crackle. 'Too much brick
and steel around us,' he said. 'If I can't hear them,
they certainly can't hear me.'

It was in the helpless silence that followed that the
voice came. It made us both jump. But, thank God, it
was Mr Megstone's voice. Though very calm and cold.

'Listen carefully. The room you are in is almost

airtight. Your air supply is strictly limited. You have enough to last about an hour.'

I glanced around wildly.

Jim nodded to a corner. 'Loudspeaker behind that grille.'

'It's all right. It's Mr Megstone,' I said. Then, like a trusting child I called out, 'Mr Megstone? It's me. Mrs Fletcher. There seems to have been some kind of mistake. We came because we were worried about you.'

'Cheshire police here, sir,' said Jim in his direst tone. 'I would advise you to release us immediately. Or else you could be in very serious trouble.'

We waited, rather anxiously. It is not a pleasant sensation to be trapped in a steel box, even when you think help is at hand.

But when the voice did come, it repeated the same message. About the air supply. In the same cold manner. With exactly the same intonation. Like the voice of the Speaking Clock. Or the voice on the Tube that tells you to stand clear of the doors.

There is no mercy in a tape recording. Any more than there is in steel walls. We waited; at the mercy of a dead machine.

You will have proved by your exertions that there is no way out of this room. Except one. By answering my questions. Please take your seat in one of the chairs provided. Again, I repeat, your supply of air is limited to one hour.

'Do as it says,' said Jim. He was still in control of

himself at this point. 'Humour it. I think it's our only chance.'

Helplessly, I sat down. The steel seat of the chair was icy cold. It seemed to be made of three-inch steel girders. And it didn't move as I sat in it, like an ordinary chair; I guessed it was bolted to the floor.

Put your ankles and wrists in the clamps provided.

I looked down. On the arms and legs of the chair were stainless steel clamps, open like the claws of a crab; thicker than handcuffs. Once they closed round my wrist or ankle . . .

You now have fifty minutes of air left.

'Do as it says, for Christ's sake,' said Jim. There was sweat dripping down his face. He pressed his wrists and ankles into the clamps, and they closed smoothly round him with tiny clicks. 'I'll put this old bastard away for life, when I lay my hands on him.'

That cheered me, somehow. Enough to put my own wrists and ankles into the clamps. When the cold bands closed around me, I could have screamed my head off. Then I noticed the yellow wires running up the chair. Electrical wires. The whole thing suddenly reminded me of an electric chair I'd seen in a TV programme about American prisoners.

Good.

There was something horrible about that mechanical approval with its slight hiss and crackle. And my cringing gratitude for it.

Good. I must warn you that you are now attached to a lie detector. If you tell lies, the moisture content of your skin will rise and I will know you are lying. Do not tell lies. I do not wish to punish you needlessly. Give me your names and addresses.

We did. Jim first, stressing the word 'constable'. Then me. Is it possible to be terrified out of your wits, and yet embarrassed at the same time? I am hopeless even with telephone answering machines.

You must speak more clearly. Do not mumble. You are not making a clear recording.

I tried again, my voice rising to a hysterical squeak. What was so obscene was that I was talking to the voice of my old friend, who gave me geraniums. But so cold, so infinitely cold that it was like a knife through my heart. Where was the *real* Mr Megstone? Why didn't he come and save me?

I will take the male first. Tell me what crimes you have committed over the last six months.

'I haven't committed any crimes,' snapped Jim. 'I'm a *policeman*.'

The next second ... it was horrible. Blue sparks

seemed to grow from his chair. His body leapt and kicked, against the clamps. From a man, he became a dancing dark blue marionette, a flailing blue dummy, not human. There was a strong smell of ozone; and what might have been burning. It seemed to go on and on. I wanted to scream; but I had no breath.

Then, at last, it stopped.

'Jim?'

He moaned. He seemed to have bitten himself, for blood was running down his chin from his mouth. I also became aware of a spreading dark stain between the legs of his uniform trousers.

'Jim? Are you all right?'

'What the hell is going on?' he said, dazed. His voice was like a lost and broken ghost. All the policeman had gone, leaving little more than a terrified animal.

Tell me what crimes you have committed in the last six months.

He began to gabble. All the peccadilloes of his harmless young life. Going for a pint after duty, when his wife was expecting him home. Sitting in a lay-by, eating toffees, when he should be on foot patrol. Using the panda to nip to the shops, wasting police petrol. His vague yen after a pretty WPC. Fiddling his expenses for going on a course. The sins got smaller and smaller, but he seemed too frightened to stop. Until finally he ran dry and wailed, like a child, 'I can't think of any more.'

Voices in the Wind

*What were you doing on the afternoon of Friday
the fifth of June?*

I heard Jim's sharply indrawn breath. That was the
day of Stephanie Harcourt's murder.

There was a long and terrifying silence, while he
struggled. It's not easy to remember what you were
doing, all those months ago. Then at last he cried out,
in a burst of boyish relief that made me want to weep,
'I was at a crime prevention meeting, at Chester. Half
a dozen of us went – Sergeant Dewsbury, Len Mostyn
– you can ask them.'

You have told the truth. Sit still and be quiet.

I think Jim must have fainted after that. I thought
at first he was dead; but then caught his chest moving
up and down.

Then it was my turn. I was lucky. I had had time
to ponder my sins. Oddly, it reminded me of the time I
was a girl, and my parents were High Church, and
I had to go to confession once a month. Now I poured
out my sins in an endless flood. Spite on the tennis
club committee. Malicious gossip. Taking advantage of
the local garage, when they undercharged for petrol. I
could not but be drearily shamed by the utter
pifflingness of it all; I was glad Jim couldn't hear it.
But I kept on ramming them down the cursed
machine's loudspeaker . . .

Enough.

Then came the question about the dreadful Friday.
'I did my ironing. And looked for my cat.'

You have told the truth. Sit still and be quiet.

The silence went on and on. Jim groaned, and came
back to himself. 'For Christ's sake, where's Megstone?
Why doesn't he come and release us?' He looked at
his watch, craning his neck. 'The bloody hour's up.
The air'll be . . .'

There was a click from the loudspeaker. At the
same moment the clamps opened. And with a long
painful rumble, the steel door slid up. We looked out,
expecting to see Megstone.

All we saw was darkness. A darkness we got out
into, pretty sharp; though Jim could hardly walk, and
I practically had to carry him.

'Where is he?' he kept mumbling. 'Where is he?
I'll kill the old bastard. I'll see they lock him in the
loony bin and throw away the key. Who does he think
he is? Who does he think he *is*? God Almighty?'

It was terrible, feeling the hate and rage running
through that weak and shaking body.

'I think he was Stephanie's father,' I said. 'Come
to avenge his daughter. Come to catch the men who
murdered her. Like rats in a trap. Stephanie said her
father lived in the Midlands, like Mr Megstone. And
her father's firm was working on a new lie detector
for the FBI . . .'

'What do you mean, he *was* Stephanie's father?
Where is he now?'

'I think he's dead. Upstairs. Can't you smell that

smell. No? Well, I used to be a nurse . . . I think he's dead but he didn't switch things off. That's why it caught us. That's why he didn't come to help us . . .'

But I don't think he was really listening. He was yelling down his radio to the police station, and getting an answer now. So I picked up his big torch, where he'd left it by the door of that room, and slowly made my way upstairs, to find my old friend.

He lay peacefully on his bed, quite cold. From the icy feel of his hand, he'd been dead some time. But, oddly, there was a smile of utter contentment on his face. He had lain down fully clothed. And he was caked with clay. Not soil, clay. Clay caked on his trousers, well above his knees. Clay caked on his shoes. Clay on his hands. Clay all over the blue bedspread, and clayey footprints on the bedroom carpet.

What had he been doing, to be digging so long and so deep? I thought I knew. I went to the bedroom window, and opened it on to his beloved back garden; her beloved back garden.

There was a spade, standing upright in the earth. And the soil of two of her rosebeds had been disturbed. In long patches.

Patches six feet long and two feet wide.

All that excitement, and dragging and digging must have brought on some kind of heart attack that had killed him.

But he must have died a happy man.

Stephanie Harcourt had been avenged.

The White Cat

Of course you all knew Kay Kingsley, the intrepid TV reporter. Kay who cycled round Bucharest with her camera crew while the Securitate were still shooting students. Kay whom President Reagan called 'sweetie-pie' at a press conference. (Much good it did him.) Kay whom Mr Gorbachev always had a smile for, no matter how bad his crises.

All my grown-up life I seem to have been seeing her, microphone in hand, against a sea of flaming vehicles. With her big blue eyes squinted up, and that tigerish grin of glee on her face. But there's one thing that I always noticed about her. She always wore a little white badge on her spotted combat jacket. And if you looked closely enough, you'd see the badge is a little white enamel cat.

I, and only I, know why she wore it. Because I was there at her beginning. At Umpleby Grammar School. I was her boyfriend. Well, sort of. More her ever-willing slave, perhaps.

We were sitting at the same table during double maths; the maths teacher was called Ellis the Trellis, because everyone saw through him so easily. I was sitting next to her, ever eager to do her bidding. It was the top maths set, because she was a bright spark even then. So was I, in those days, even though I later became a chartered accountant.

Anyway, on this particular day, I noticed she was staring at the ceiling. Mind you, we all stared at the ceiling during double maths in search of inspiration, solace, or merely escape. But usually everybody else's eyes were out of focus. Kay's, however, on this occasion, were as sharp as needles. She was actually *watching* something.

I followed her eye, to see what she was staring at. There were the usual damp stains on the ceiling, that looked like maps of South Island New Zealand, or Tierra del Fuego. The only other thing was a hatch in the ceiling, a wire grille set in a surround of shiny brown wood, about as exciting as having your hair cut. But it was that that she was staring at. With great intentness.

'What's up wi' you?' I hissed. I was afraid that the boredom of Ellis the Trellis's lessons had finally driven her nuts. I was scared that one of the other lads would notice, and nobody likes their girlfriend being called nuts. I mean, you might have to bash somebody for it. Even someone bigger than yourself.

'There's something up there,' she whispered. 'Behind the grille. Something white. It keeps on coming and going.'

'Bit of waste paper,' I hissed, 'blowing in the draught.'

'No,' she said. 'It's *watching* me.'

I broke out in a cold sweat. Ellis the Trellis must have really blown her mind this time. I contemplated the third-year equivalent of divorce, which was sitting at somebody else's table.

Anyway, just then the bell went; and Ellis the Trellis fled to the staff room before we lynched him, and the rest of the set went after him like the usual herd of elephants.

'C'mon,' I said gruffly, to distract her. 'Let's go to the tuck shop. I'll buy you a Mars Bar.' I was down to my last thirty p, but love is love.

'No,' she said, putting her chair on the table beneath the hatch in the ceiling. 'I'm going to find out what it is.' She got up on the chair, and pushed at the hatch. It moved, revealing darkness. And then, of all things, the head of a small white cat peered down at her, ears pricked.

I was so glad she wasn't crazy.

The cat sniffed her fingers, tentatively. Then, when she tried to grab it, it moved back into the darkness like greased lightning, the way cats do.

'I'm going up after it,' she said. 'It might be trapped up there. It might be *starving*.'

'For God's sake,' I said. 'It's nearly bell-time. We're due in N14 for geography. We can report it to the caretaker.'

'No,' she said. 'He might take it to be put down or anything. I'm going up.' And she put her hands round the edge of the hatch and heaved herself halfway through.

And then the bell went. She was stuck.

'Help me, Stan,' came her muffled plea. 'Push my bum.'

I pushed – and she vanished with a last sexy wriggle which I still remember to this day.

I whipped the grille cover back in place just as the Fifth came piling in, led by Mr Jameson, the history master; who did not like me. And there I was, standing alone with my head against the ceiling.

'Ho,' says Jameson. 'There you are, Timpson! Practising to join the circus? You should have a good career there. As one of the performing baboons no doubt!'

The fifth year loved that.

Well, I got through double geography somehow. Even managed to keep a straight face and tell the geography teacher that Kay was lying down in the girls' sick room with a bad headache; the one place where every man fears to go. He got his own back by giving me fifty lines for not paying attention. Not paying attention? Crikey, I was going mad. She might asphyxiate up there, or come crashing through the plaster ceiling and break a leg.

Never was I so grateful to hear the school bell for the end of the day. I dashed back to the maths room. There wasn't a sound from the hatch.

'Come down for God's sake!' I bellowed at the ceiling.

I waited for nearly an hour and a half, nearly at my wit's end, convinced that she was dead.

It was at this point that Kay Kingsley walked in through the *door*, dusty as hell and grinning her head off.

'What the . . . why the . . .?'

'Don't have a fit,' she said, 'come and have a Coke. I'm buying.'

She swung her legs sitting on the wall outside the newsagent's and pulled the ring off her Coke can.

'I came down through the hatch in the girls' toilets,' she said cheerfully. 'Seemed the safest place. The roof space all joins up, and there's a hatch in the ceiling of every room. Must be a ventilation system.'

'But what took you so *long*?'

'Oh, Stan, it was so *fascinating* up there. I couldn't tear myself away.'

'Oh, very fascinating, I'm sure,' I said sarcastically. 'Spiders and cobwebs, dust and dead flies. What do you want to be when you grow up? The Mummy's Curse?'

'Well, there was the cat. Though she wouldn't let me catch her, and soon shot off, through a broken ventilator in the wall over the bike sheds. I never saw her again.'

'So . . .?'

'Well, you can look down into all the rooms, and watch people without being seen, and hear what they are saying. Did you know the head practises putting with a golf club in his study? Into the waste basket? And talks to himself while he's doing it, pretending to be Nick Faldo?'

That pinned my ears back.

'And I think Mr Chambers and Miss Ramsden are in *love*. They stayed in the staff room after the rest had left, and were holding hands and whispering sweet nothings to each other.'

173

'But Mr Chambers is married. His wife and kids came to Sports Day . . .'

'The secrets of all hearts shall be revealed,' she said, with a wink. 'I'm going to start a gossip column in the school newspaper.'

The school newspaper was a crummy inky thing run by a bunch of sixth formers. In a school of eight hundred, it sold about fifty copies, because people just borrowed it off those foolish enough to actually buy it. I mean, it cost the price of half a Mars Bar. But the moment Kay's Kolumn, as it was called, began to be published, the circulation trebled. She spent a lot of time up in the roof space, though now she used the hatch in the girls' toilets most of the time, which kept me out of it.

She never overplayed her hand; but she got some rare scoops. She forecast the parents were going to buy us a swimming bath; and it happened. She was the first with the news that Rogerson had been chosen to play in the North of England trials at rugby. She gave us the news that Mr Chambers and Miss Ramsden were going to organize a long school trip to the Loire Valley châteaux next summer. Mr Chambers and Miss Ramsden walked around the school looking very pale and sweaty for days, and she said they gave her very funny looks . . .

But she never overplayed her hand. She always started off any forecast with her famous phrase 'rumour hath it that'. And the staff, who were very put out at having so much of their business known, just thought that other members of staff had opened their big mouths too much too soon.

Until the fatal day that she came to me absolutely boiling over with rage and indignation.

'I've just heard the head talking to Rodney Tillotson's father on the phone. The head's going to make Rodney Tillotson head boy next year, because Father Tillotson's promised him a thousand quid for the minibus fund.'

'But Tillotson's a *weed*,' I said. 'He'll never get a grip. The school will be a *shambles*. There'll be riots!'

'I know,' she said, and that was when I first saw her eyes form those famous slits, and her face adopt that famous tigerish grin. 'And I'm going to stop it. And I need your help. I can't do it alone.'

'Why me?' I stammered, suddenly utterly terrified.

'I've got to get it into the school newspaper,' she said. 'Without the sixth-form editors reading it first. Without *anybody* reading it first.'

'How can you do that?'

'This fortnight's paper is lying in the school office, ready for duplicating...'

'And...?'

'We're going to have to burgle the school after dark. We can climb up on to the bike-shed roof and get into the roof space through that broken ventilator. The way the white cat gets in. Then we drop down into the secretary's office... It'll be as easy as pie... but you'll have to be there, to give me a leg up afterwards. Then I can pull you up after me.'

I nearly had a fit. But Kay could get a look of contempt on her face and I knew that if I refused, I'd be out in the cold for good. And besides, Rodney Tillotson was *such* a weed, and I admired Ben Scott, who should have been made head boy, or so everybody thought . . .

'OK,' I said.

'*Tonight*,' she said, with her tiger-look. 'Meet you at half past seven at the youth club.'

I was glad it was that night. If I'd had to wait longer, I'm sure I'd have jumped in the river.

As it turned out, it was fatally easy. Nobody saw us go up over the bike-shed roof, or through the broken ventilator. And she knew her way by feel through the roof space, though I almost put my foot through a couple of ceilings, in my nervousness. But I shall never forget the moment when we got the grille off the hatch in the secretary's office, and I shone down my pencil torch into the holy of holies.

'It looks so different from up here . . .' I muttered.

'*Everything* looks so different from up here,' she said. 'I haven't seen the world the same at all, since the white cat first showed me all this. Everything in the world has got a polite face, that they show you down *there*. And everything's got another face, when you peep from up here. The things I've heard the men staff say about me . . .'

That made me mad then; that the men staff should talk about her so, even if she did have a smashing figure for her age, the best in the third year. And that rage gave me the courage to jump down, on to the secretary's desk.

It didn't take long. She riffled through the pages of the typed-up newspaper, and soon found a little gap at the bottom of a page. She shoved it into the secretary's typewriter and typed:

THE HEAD IS GOING TO MAKE RODNEY TILLOTSON HEAD BOY NEXT YEAR. TILLOTSON'S FATHER IS GIVING A THOUSAND POUNDS TO THE MINIBUS FUND.

And then she put the sheets back as they had been, ready for the photocopier. The sentence just looked like all the other typing. The secretary would never notice. The sixth formers stapling up the sheets would never notice. Nobody would, until they read it.

Then we went back the way we came. Nobody saw us at all. We went back to the youth club, to give ourselves an alibi. And to drink Coke and dance. She danced for me alone that night. On her doorstep, she kissed me. I walked home; my feet hardly touched the ground.

Rodney Tillotson never made head boy. And they didn't get that thousand quid for the minibus fund. But teachers are not fools, whatever you say. They found the faint imprint of my trainers on the school secretary's blotting pad. And they looked up and saw our dusty fingerprints on the shiny wooden surround of the ceiling grille. And then they found our footprints in the dust in the roof space.

Or rather the prints of *my* trainers, to be precise. For my dad had bought me them on our camping trip to France, and the patterns on the soles were like no others in the school.

And then Jameson must have told them about finding me doing my circus act under the grille in the maths room . . .

I was on the head's carpet, and there were about five of them staring at me like I was a Nazi war criminal. And it wasn't just a matter of being expelled. There was talk of charges of burglary, and charges of criminal libel. And I was close to tears, thinking what it would do to my parents when they heard . . .

And then in bounced Kay, with that tigerish look set so hard on her face that I don't think it ever really came off ever again. And she started on about the things she'd seen from her roof space, and the things she'd heard. She really gave it to them . . . she'd hardly started when I was sent out of the room. I suppose they thought the things weren't fit for my ears.

She didn't come out of there until the bell went for home time. Then she just jerked her head at me and said, 'C'mon, let's get out of here. I'll buy you a Coke.'

We went and sat in the park, where it was peaceful. She swung her legs in triumph, and said, 'You're off the hook, Stan. You are merely the innocent dupe, led on by a wicked scheming young hussy. I'm the ringleader. It's only the ringleaders they ever really want. You just go back to school tomorrow, and keep your mouth shut, and you won't hear any more about it.'

'But you . . .?'

'There are plenty of other schools. My father can afford to pay for a private one, where they'll take anybody if you pay enough. He'll probably send me off to a boarding school, as far away as possible.'

'Shan't . . . shan't I ever see you again?'

'Better not, Stan. For you, I'm *trouble*.'

'I wish I was like you, Kay.'

'But you're not, Stan. If you can't stand the heat, stay out of the kitchen . . . be a chartered accountant or something.'

'But shan't I *ever* see you again?' I wasn't just saying goodbye to my first love; it was like saying goodbye to a goddess . . .

She smiled. 'Oh, I think you'll see me again. If you go on watching the news long enough. There's two sides to this world. The front side and the back side. I'm going to show the world its own back side . . . There's nothing else I can do now. Since that little white cat showed me the back side, I can't look at anything else. I'm doomed, Stan, *doomed*.'

And with a wave of the hand, she was gone out of my life for ever.

Except, I watched the news for her. And, ten years later, there she was in Belfast, against her favourite backdrop of burning cars. Digging away at the RUC's shoot-to-kill policy.

That was when I sent her the little white cat badge . . . which she always wore on her combat jacket after that. She sent me a handmade badge in return; it must have cost her a packet.

The sole of a trainer; in red and gold.

Last week, as you know, she copped it in Beirut; a sniper's bullet, in some stupid little square full of wrecked concrete buildings. Still digging for the truth. Doomed, as she said herself.

They say she was buried wearing the white cat; nobody knew where the famous white cat had come from.

Except me.

Robert Westall
Ghosts and Journeys

*A thing like a shrivelled hand . . . like a great thin grey spider .
. . crawled out from under the cupboard. Everyone saw it
quite clearly. And all the rest of their lives they would never
forget it . . .*

A bus carries a cargo of the dead on a journey into the past.
A mirror's curse traps a cheating lover. A frightened
schoolgirl inflicts punishment from beyond the grave . . .

The power of the paranormal takes control in a world where
nothing is as it seems. Six dark and chilling stories from the
brilliant imagination of a great writer.

Robert Westall
The Promise

'Promise that if I ever get lost, you'll come and find me.'

Valerie was beautiful, with her long red hair and her pale, pale face. Bob found it easy to promise her anything. And he meant it, too.

But now Valerie is dying. And she's stronger in death than she was in life. Bob finds himself facing a force more powerful than anything he's ever known - a love that survives the grave; a promise that never dies . . .

A terrifying love story from the master of the supernatural.

Robert Westall
Rachel and the Angel

She felt the heat of the thing on her face, even from this distance. It was glowing like a black cage of fire, like a volcano about to erupt.

Rachel had imagined angels to be beautiful and good. This creature was terrifying - and bent on destruction . . .

The sins of a whole town are about to be punished . . . A child lures an old man to his death on Christmas Eve . . . An ancient tomb brings catastrophic powers to an unsuspecting farmer.

Six strange tales of the bizarre, the disturbing and the unexpected, to haunt the dark recesses of your mind.

Robert Westall titles
available from Macmillan

The prices shown below are correct at the time of going to press.
However, Macmillan Publishers reserve the right to show new retail
prices on covers which may differ from those previously advertised.

ROBERT WESTALL

Blitzcat	0 330 31040 2	£3.99
The Cats of Seroster	0 330 29239 0	£3.99
Fathom Five	0 330 32230 3	£3.99
The Machine-Gunners	0 330 33428 X	£3.99
A Time of Fire	0 330 33754 8	£3.99
The Haunting of Chas McGill	0 330 34065 4	£3.99
The Watch House	0 330 33571 5	£3.99
The Devil on the Road	0 330 34064 6	£3.99
Ghosts and Journeys	0 330 30904 8	£3.99
A Place for Me	0 330 33427 1	£3.99
The Promise	0 330 31741 5	£3.99
Rachel and the Angel	0 330 30235 3	£3.99
Voices in the Wind	0 330 35218 0	£3.99
The Wind Eye	0 330 32234 6	£3.99
Yaxley's Cat	0 330 32499 3	£3.99

All Macmillan titles can be ordered at your local bookshop
or are available by post from:

Book Service by Post
PO Box 29, Douglas, Isle of Man IM99 1BQ

Credit cards accepted. For details:
Telephone: 01624 675137
Fax: 01624 670923
E-mail: bookshop@enterprise.net

Free postage and packing in the UK.
Overseas customers: add £1 per book (paperback)
and £3 per book (hardback).